MW00624960

# MAYLIS DE KERANGAL

# Canoes

TRANSLATED FROM THE FRENCH BY
Jessica Moore

*archipelago books*

Copyright © Maylis de Kerangal, 2021
English translation copyright © Jessica Moore, 2024
Originally published as *Canoës* by Éditions Gallimard, Paris, 2021

First Archipelago Books Edition, 2024

All rights reserved. No part of this book may be reproduced or transmitted in
any form without the prior written permission of the publisher.

Library of Congress Cataloging-in-Publication
Data available upon request.
ISBN 9781953861962

Archipelago Books
232 3rd Street #A111
Brooklyn, NY 11215
www.archipelagobooks.org

Distributed by Penguin Random House
www.penguinrandomhouse.com

Cover art: Vivian Maier
This work is made possible by the New York State Council
on the Arts with the support of the Office of the Governor
and the New York State Legislature.

This publication was made possible with support from
the Carl Lesnor Family Foundation, the Hawthornden Foundation,
the New York City Department of Cultural Affairs and the
National Endowment for the Arts.

PRINTED IN CANADA

# CANOES

# Contents

# Bivouac

I LAY THERE waiting for time to pass, tipped back to horizontal in the dentist's chair, my eyes roving over the Styrofoam drop ceiling, my feet up, and my teeth sunk into an alginate-based, fluoride-flavored paste. The clamor of the boulevard reached me from far off, the young practitioner standing behind me clinked the tools on her tray, and I could trace a thin stream of Middle Eastern music in this little primeval chaos while the mold hardened. And so, my mouth was full and I was concentrating on not swallowing when the dentist came up to me and held her phone up to my eyes: look, a human jawbone from the mesolithic, they found it in the 15th arrondissement, rue Henry-Farman, in 2008.

On the screen, lit up against a black background like a precious object, I distinctly recognized a jaw, a bone that still had four molars in their sockets. The chin was protruding, expressing something like an appetite, a strength, a will. Good teeth, even if worn. The jaw is very important, the dentist continued in a reedy voice, slipping the phone into her shirt pocket, it's the only mobile bone in the face, and speaking, eating, seeing well, or even standing upright and balanced – all of this concerns the jaw. Our whole organism is suspended from this see-saw.

I closed my eyes. For a few months now, dizziness and migraines had been wreaking havoc on my life. They could come on at any time, breaking and entering without warning – headaches usually at the end of the day. I tried to note the commonalities in their onset, whether lack of sleep, too much alcohol, some upset, but couldn't find a pattern and had become a woman on high alert, vulnerable, precarious. Yesterday once again, in the middle of the afternoon while I was working on the urgent and badly paid translation of subtitles for an entire season of the series *Out into the Open* – six runaway teenagers survive in a forest in Oregon – I felt the pain quiver in my temple, furtive at first, nearly clandestine, but sly and (I knew from experience) capable of inflaming my whole head in the space of a single second. And yet – the apartment was bathed in a thick silence, full of the resonance of familiar rooms in the off hours, when they're deserted, deactivated, like abandoned base camps, and then indecipherable forms rise up, reliefs, strange traces that we contemplate at length. Twenty minutes later, I was flat on my back in the dark.

Shall we begin? The dentist looked at her watch and readjusted her blue mask, her eyes above it like a Persian cat's, and then I opened wide and she leaned over to remove the mold from my upper jaw, jiggling the handle of the metal form below my palate vigorously – her force surprised me, I felt like my teeth were going to be pulled right out. When the mold emerged she examined it at length, turning it this way and that under the light, and then she nodded, satisfied, as I spat out little pebbles of pink paste into a bowl. Great, now we'll do the same for the bottom jaw. She moved through the room, agile in her red sneakers, digitigrade gait and slender dancer's waist, braid like a metronome, then perched on a stool beside the chair and prepared another batch of alginate cut with water on her tray, concentrating. I wiped my chin with paper towel. Where was the prehistoric jawbone? I heard myself ask – the words rolling from my lips like more little pebbles, final crumbs of pink paste – as I watched her slender arms working, round and muscled, covered in freckles. One sec, we'll have a look after. She got up, stuffed the full mold back into my mouth – a purée with a squeaky texture – and I listened to her rinse her hands at the sink before she answered my question in her clear voice: it was rue Henry-Farman, near the Paris heliport, metro Balard.

My eyes wandered towards the drop ceiling once more, and I began to visualize the meander of the Seine near Boulogne, the islands, the ring road, while these three names, Farman, heliport, Balard – quick-setting names like the paste – resonated in my temples, bringing back the neighborhood where Olive Formose had lived, her apartment where I spent three days when I was thirteen; and, progressively, the grid of Styrofoam tiles above me became no more than a vast confluence, their light, flaky relief a zone of encounters and troubles, where memories formed whirlwinds like undertows.

I sometimes called her Aunt Olive, and she didn't like it when I did: Olive Formose was not my aunt but a friend of my mother's who had gone to live in Paris after the death of her fiancé in a helicopter accident in the Port of Le Havre. I must have been three or four then. All I knew about her was that she lived alone, didn't have any children, and worked in television: very little, in short, but powerful pieces of data – tragedy and show business, solitude – which sketched the contours of an intriguing feminine figure, intimate and close, although no one could be further from my known world. Olive never came to see us, telephoned only rarely, and yet every year my mother went to Paris to spend a few days with her. She never missed this visit, which would certainly have required, I realize now, a fair amount of organization, including negotiating her absence with my father, my brothers becoming unmanageable the day before she left, and me listless, distant. I was quite happy to make things difficult for her – though I loved being the daughter of a woman who went to see her friend in Paris, and if she hadn't been able to leave, it would have been my undoing as well, still, it was stronger than me: beside Olive (I saw them in photos posed together in unknown places, laughing and legendary, cigarettes dangling, legs tanned and hair wild), my mother became someone else, a rare, mysterious woman, and I was jealous of this mystery.

One day in November, on All Saints' Day, I'm the one who's leaving. I cross the station in Le Havre like a queen, wearing a crimson wool gabardine coat belted at the waist, Levi's, and new sneakers, hands clutching the handles of a leather-trimmed canvas travel bag, and I don't even look back at my siblings who've come to see me off, envious, seething, moaning over their lot while I prepare to escape. Olive is there to meet me at the end of the track, smaller and older than in my memory, wearing pleated slacks, a Prince of Wales kimono jacket, and a black beret. She smiles at me with red lips, her head tilted to the side, and I can tell she's examining me, you're tall for your age, it's getting dark, we board the metro, I memorize the names of the stations on the line until we reach the last stop and get off, a bistro on place Balard, I hope you're hungry, the lights ricochet off the gold tubing of the counters, I don't take my eyes off her, the server has a cleft lip and calls her Miss Olive, I order the steak-frîtes and a chocolate mousse, she dines on a poached egg and an Irish coffee, after which we crowd into the narrow elevator, the two-room apartment on the top floor is open to the night sky, and, far off, the Seine lies shimmering. Olive pours herself a whisky and leans her forehead against the bay window for a long moment. I'm glad to get to know you. There's a sleeping bag on the living room sofa, I lay my head on a batik cushion, lights sweep across the ceiling, bluish haloes move over the walls: I'm sleeping under the stars. *Out into the Open.* In the night, I hear helicopters.

The helicopter had exploded the instant one of the rotor blades touched the water, and her fiancé, who was piloting, disintegrated in the atmosphere, his body's matter pulverized, scattered over the surface of the sea, drifting to the bottom of the impenetrable Channel. Heat and dust. I sometimes caught her following the flight of civil security helicopters over the ring road with her eyes and talking to herself, leaving a halo of steam on the windowpane – I wondered if she was hearing a voice. We ate all our meals at the bistro – she didn't cook at all – went to the movies at Odéon in the evenings, and one morning, she took me with her to the TV station. The high life. On my last day, at the end of the afternoon, thunder rumbled, lightning sheared the sky, and the windows trembled. It's your last night. We had a drink of strong alcohol, a toast. I had grown up. My center of gravity had shifted a few centimeters.

Yoo-hoo! Three minutes is up, we're taking out the mold. I open my eyes to the Styrofoam sky where helicopters dance. The dentist is above me, very close – her pendant, a small gold metal canoe, dangles beside my nose. We're almost finished here, I'll release you in a sec.

Later, she fills out different forms – estimate, bill, treatment plan – and I scan the room, my eyes stopping on a few dental molds piled in a corner between promotional pens and other freebies from laboratories; I'm immediately disturbed by these strange replicas in blue, pink, or grey plaster, these mute and lonely human jaws lying there as though extracted from their skeletons, some of them tense and gritting their teeth, while others, wide open, seem to be screaming at the top of their lungs. Absent-mindedly, I begin massaging my jaw: fingers at my temples rub the ball of the joint, palpate the bone at the base of my ear, knead my cheeks. The dentist mentions a follow-up appointment and the potential benefit of a temporomandibular scan, but her voice is far away now, I can't take my eyes off these plaster reproductions, so precise, so detailed – a miniscule space between two molars, the serrated edge of an incisor, a groove on the enamel of a canine – that they are filled with presence, each correlated to a unique being, a person who came here and lay in this same chair, anxious perhaps, with their particular mouth problem. And now I can make out the names written in pencil on the bases of the molds, and I remember that it's the study of teeth, whether in isolated cases or mass disasters, that sometimes offers the only possibility for formal identification, as reliable as genetic or digital prints – Olive, wearing a thin bottle-green cardigan that shows her clavicle and the palpitations of her fragile neck: he had no burial, they didn't find anything that might identify him, no remains, no medal, not even a tooth.

The appointment is almost over. The dentist held out the papers one by one, summing up everything, professional, I handed her my Health Card and credit card, and now I'm putting things back in my bag, ready to break camp, but she's not moving: I can't see what she's looking at on her computer as her expression changes. She frowns. Her fingers click the mouse, and then her face lights up as she turns the screen toward me, with the photo of the mandible again, the great relic, and together, suddenly close, shoulder to shoulder above her desk, we read out loud: on the banks of an old arm of the Seine, nomads, the last hunter-gatherers of prehistory, set up their camp; hunting stations, bivouacs; they stopped here many times, treated game, cut up meat, tanned hides, whittled arrowheads, leaving behind traces that archaeologists would bring to light ten thousand years later, over the course of months spent kneeling on the ground – traces of flint and sandstone, animal remains, evidence of a fire pit, and a little way away, isolated near a fragment of femur, this old mouth on the ground with its four teeth, this human bone that persists, this debris which nothing has overcome, not the earth, not the river, not even ten thousand years of land use and conquest of the sky. We don't know if it's linked to a burial plot. Staring at this jaw without a voice, I wonder how these men and women talked, I want to hear them. Today, a household-waste sorting center stands in the spot of the 2008 archaeological dig.

The dentist gets up, walks around her desk, and I follow her movement, in sync and steady on my feet. When we reach the doorway, she says again that an unbalanced bite could definitely be causing my migraines and vertigo, and she holds out a hand that I take, my mind elsewhere, drawn to those plaster jaws pushed into a corner, those mute and fragile mouths like improperly fitted reed valves, and I'm thinking of my own, which doesn't close properly, and which will soon join the others.

# Stream and Iron Filings

**M**Y NEW radio arrived tonight, a beautiful orange vintage Optalix. I admired it from all angles, and the instant I put the batteries in, it began spitting out its iron filings – sharp little sounds like arrowheads shot by some miniature sadistic archer hidden inside the casing. I found the notched knob on the side and turned it feverishly to flush out an audible frequency on the FM band. I felt like I was crossing another dimension of reality in a breaststroke, immersed in the crackling of electromagnetic waves, when a human voice emerged from the depths against the soundtrack of a tropical forest: . . . *scientific observations* *have established that chimpanzees and rhesus macaques lower their pitch during altercations to signal to the other members of the group that they are ready to fight, to protect their resources, and to assert their status.* I stopped the red line, listened to the recorded cries of the primates and the sounding of the tree canopy, and then the program was over – a woman's voice, slightly husky and with a masculine tessitura, greeted listeners and announced that tonight would be the longest night of the year.

Now, instead of going to sleep, I'm drifting: the vocal modulations of chimpanzees and rhesus monkeys, radio voices that blur gender, and the night like a sound reflector, all of this brings back that freezing day in December, a Friday, when I saw Zoé again after a long stretch of time (with no other cause than a reciprocal negligence), a date we'd agreed to by text, thus avoiding the blandness of blaming stressful lives in Western megacities, lack of space, and time that flies.

Legend has it that true friends are those who know how to reconnect in an instant, to meet again "as though they had seen each other just yesterday," and that evening, when Zoé appeared on the terrasse of the Babylonian Café, splendid in a black peacoat, Turkey-red lipstick and matching boots, this was the feeling I had at first: here she is. I watched her slalom between tables, caught in the reddish halo of the heat lamps, and sit down like a flower. We ordered two White Russians right away and clinked our glasses, looking each other in the eye, reunions require it. And yet, sitting there before our cocktails of cream and vodka, and even though we certainly saw ourselves as solid friends, instead of spitting it out immediately, we skated over a sham of platitudes, nonchalant small talk with the sole function, we both knew it, of acting like a guy rope on the situation, putting off the moment when we would finally talk.

So, have I changed? Her eyes stirred in mine like silver-fish. Prelude over, I thought. I would have liked to have given a waxed-canvas response, light, to have said airily, "everyone changes," as I picked up another olive from the Moroccan bowl, but in fact, Zoé sat there like a doppelgänger of herself, without me being able to identify where the dissonance lay – I felt like I was feverishly turning the knob on the side of a transistor radio so as to stop hearing iron filings, and to find the right station for my friend.

Caught off guard, I latched onto her way of smoking – wrist bent and cigarette dangling between thumb and index – her way of biting the inside of her cheeks in bemusement, or how she tossed her hair back. I was relieved to recognize her, sunny, passionate, and ambitious when she spoke about her new job at the radio, where she hoped eventually to be on the air. But an invisible difference was interfering with her presence, altering the image of her that I'd formed over all these years. It was only when she answered a phone call and stepped away from me, turning her back, that I realized Zoé was talking differently. Her voice – in other words, the singular vibration she emitted in the atmosphere and which I would have recognized as hers among thousands of others – was no longer in her body and seemed dubbed by someone else, just barely different, but different all the same. Your voice, I said, stroking my throat involuntarily, your voice has changed. Zoé sat up straighter: you think? I nodded, and a victorious grin appeared immediately at her mouth like a tennis player who's just landed a decisive point: cool! Seeing my surprise, she explained: I don't want my shitty voice anymore.

What Zoé called her shitty voice was nothing other than a clear and lively timbre, a voice with a staccato flow, sharp, but one that could grow louder without stridence – a mountain stream. I like that voice, it's hers. When I think of Zoé, this is the timbre that comes to mind and, in its wake, I remember the night she sang American folk songs: we were camping in Aubrac, canoes in the grass, it was summer, the tent amplified her song like an Andalusian patio, Zoé's voice was crystal clear, and the silence between each sound was dense as platinum.

But it seems this voice was too high to become a radio voice. We don't really like sugary little voices here, Zoé had recently been told, a way of warning her that her access to the microphone was compromised and that she'd do better to take her dreams down a notch. She heard this portent as an incitement to prove her worth, to show that she was persistent, and above all, to work on her voice in order to make it lower, deeper, calmer. More masculine, you mean? I asked. Less feminine in any case, she retorted, lighting a smoke. So Zoé went in search of her low voice, the one that connotes all the competence, authority, and assurance no one would grant her high voice. Every week she went to a vocal coach who taught her how to lower her frequency, because it's not easy with high voices, you know, they don't do as well on the radio, it's technical, it's linked to the human ear, we have to think of the listeners. The coach, a highly qualified individual, had clearly comforted her with the idea that her voice was, if not a shitty voice, at least at a natural disadvantage: that of women, because the higher your voice, the more people perceive you as fragile, nervous, weak – and in contrast, the lower your voice, the more you're judged to be solid, reassuring, and trustworthy, you see? I nodded, pursing my lips in disapproval – in my mind there was nothing "natural" about all this, but Zoé said it was true, women's voices had become lower in the last fifty years, ever since they had started occupying positions of power: it's scientifically proven. And as though to celebrate this social shift, this female voice break, a revolution, we ordered two more White Russians.

The terrasse had filled up, it was spilling over now onto the sidewalk, drowned in the din of people just beginning their Friday night, but now everything was happening as though Zoé and I had recreated the tent from the hiking trip in Aubrac, the textile capsule where my friend had sung all night, hymns for women who were independent and proud. I remembered then the men with their white legs covered in bug bites who had undertaken the first studies on primates and, captivated as they were by the males' behavior (alpha males, super males), completely missed the essential – they ignored the role of the females. These researchers observed the social life of the great apes through the prism of the society in which they themselves moved. It wasn't until a young woman came to observe the chimpanzees and sat down among them in the tall grasses – a blond woman with a delicate, slow, and incredibly sure voice – that the complexity of their world was understood.

I started to speak again, slowly: these women's voices that get lower and closer to men's, is this good news? Zoé had pushed back from the table so as to better frame me in her focus, face kindled under the lights, and spoke as though to a stubborn child you're trying to convince without forcing, yes, she said, enunciating each syllable, doing away with the boo boop dee do little-girl voice – she imitated Marilyn's singing – the high, whispery voice that's trying to seduce, the sweet voice that wants to be protected, getting rid of the tiny voice whose purpose is to reassure the large male one, while never disturbing his power or challenging his place – each time she said the word "voice" she punctuated it with a nod, without taking her eyes off me – the voice that's there to soften, to tone down, to charm: to be finished with this masquerade of the feminine voice, *yes, this masquerade*, is good news. She ran a hand through her hair, she was clear and determined, but something in me resisted, rejected the assimilated superiority of the low voice, the bogus technical arguments, the maxims of the highly qualified vocal coach, and the idea of having to change one's voice simply in order to have the right to take action.

I listened to Zoé. I didn't want her voice to ape that of a man with white legs covered in bug bites, I didn't want her voice to be swallowed up in iron filings, and I didn't want the vibrations of her tiny vocal cords, which testified to her living presence in the world, to be part of a threatened biodiversity – must all the mountain streams dry up? Around us, the terrasse was thinning out, quieting, the night carrying on elsewhere, at other parties, but the orangey glow of the heat lamps still colored our cheeks, and the stars twinkled up there in the icy sky; the moment had come for us to sing together, and we ordered two more White Russians.

# Mustang

*A leaf a gourd a shell a net a bag a sling a sack*
*a bottle a pot a box a container. A holder. A recipient.*
—Ursula K. Le Guin, "The Carrier Bag
Theory of Fiction" (1986)

I GRAB the neck of a dinosaur with long lashes and the hand of a small boy with dark-chocolate eyes, put them both in the car, half my body engulfed by the back seat, torso twisted, fingers straining to reach, and then fasten the seatbelt. I put a multicoloured backpack containing lunch in a plastic box, a bag of chips, a bottle of water, and a change of clothes, size 5T, on the seat beside them. Then I walk back around the car, keys bouncing against my palm, sit down behind the wheel, and start the car. First Tuesday in December, mid-1990s, it's 8:30 a.m., bitterly cold, and blue is the color of the sky.

We're on time leaving for school. Easy clothes, black coffee and corn flakes, fried eggs, mint toothpaste: we've checked the boxes, spatial and temporal, that measure out the first hour of the morning, these signposts that, like stakes for plant stems, prevent the day from derailing before it's even begun. While I help Kid get dressed – lumberjack shirt with red and black squares, jeans, and sneakers: a real little American – Sam makes his lunch, careful to peel the apple and cut the sandwiches into triangles. Then he grabs his jacket and kisses my neck on the fly, hops on his bike, and rides off to campus. I zip up Kid's coat and kiss him on the nose. Let's go. In the next minute, just as we're walking out the door, I pause like a plane on the tarmac before lift-off, take a deep breath, and squint into the icy sun, the air smells like wet earth and hops from the Coors made at the brewery nearby, and I still take a moment to let the scene sink in a little, lightly lifted from myself, it's true, ever since I came to live here, in Golden, Colorado.

I look at Kid in the rearview mirror: Yumiko's coming today with her dog, remember? He turns his face to the window without answering. I go on: you'll see Tom, you'll see Oona and Lazlo, and you'll get to meet Yumiko's dog. Silence. Kid is concentrating, he's on the alert. The home of *la souris verte*,[1] the green mouse, should be appearing soon in the continuum of lawns and houses scrolling past, portrait gallery of the white American middle class, Christian, hardworking, the Star-Spangled Banner flying from the balcony, XXL cartons of ice cream at the back of the freezer, and the gun stored flat in the night-table drawer. I like taking stock of these similar façades, all facing the same way, each house camped on a parcel of land enclosed by nothing, no fence, no hedge, no gate or clothesline, the front yard landscaped but the back in shambles, all single story but detached, so grass

1. "Une souris verte" (A green mouse) is one of the most well-known nursery rhymes for children in France.

grows between them and brings back the great prairie of beginnings, the one that carries the song of the dawn. Suddenly Kid's face lights up and he lets out a shout, pointing out a light-green house, the green mouse! I nod, laughing: okay, you win! We sing the famous children's song at the top of our lungs while the frieze of doors, windows, and rooftops files past, garages and lawnmowers, all of it stretched out like a repertoire of forms, an endless market aisle in which I seek out, from the corner of my eye, one that looks like me – I am an American house, the front yard landscaped, the back a mess, and all around me a prairie grows: just like in the song, I am a green mouse lost in the grass.

It's a straight shot south all the way to school, nothing could be simpler. The roads are still rectilinear here, they cross each other at right angles. It's only once you're past the downtown, laid out like a checkerboard, and back in the grasslands or winding along the side of a mountain that they find their undulations again, like locks of hair escaped from a rigid braid. We're almost there.

The houses are bigger now and more spaced out. In the rearview mirror, Kid is imperturbable. You okay? He nods, mouth set in an ictal pout. Are you glad you'll get to meet Yumiko's dog? Silence. The school appears on the left on South Golden Road, behind the pines, between the greyish building of a giant Chinese restaurant open 24-7 and an aseptic horse-riding club, on one of the first curves past the city. It's a varnished pine house with a grassy lawn enclosed by a fence. It's Davy Crockett's cabin. I park the car in front and turn to my little boy: so, what did you decide? Is Dino coming with you, or will he stay in the car? With me. Awkward gymnastics to unbuckle Kid and I emerge from the car with my lumbar and cervical vertebrae aching, then the three of us are on the front step, ringing the doorbell. The teachers meet us on the wooden porch, welcoming, positive, continuous babble of nasal voices and enthusiastic exclamations. I note that one of them, Lizzie, is dressed up as a milk cow – a prime Holstein: she's wearing a white suit with large black spots complete with an imposing udder in pink plastic sewn on at the crotch and a tail in the back. Today is Milky Day, she smiles at me, a toothy smile, unremitting, and she repeats Milky Day as she looks deep into my eyes, her upper lip pulled back above pink gums, making sure I understand the English words. Inside I'm thinking, damn it, milky day! Today all the activities will revolve around the themes of cows, farms, the calcium that fortifies the bones of little Americans and the teeth of Lizzie the teacher. Yumiko's dog is tomorrow, I got it wrong. I kiss my son. Bye sweetie! Sam will pick you up. Do you want to say bye to me, too? His beautiful dark eyes stare up at me, two impenetrable licorice candies, and I wait, hesitate, kiss him again, his hair smells like dry hay and mandarin oranges, then he turns, tosses Dino into my arms and runs off to join the others. You'll see, children can adapt to everything, people kept telling me before we left. You too – you'll adapt.

The sky whitens rapidly, they're calling for snow today. Kid's dinosaur is on the passenger seat – I brought it with me. I could turn around and take it back to the school, but I've already set off, I won't backtrack now: the day opens, dilates, and these hours belong to me – an influx of time that throws me off balance, a storm in a garden. When it comes down to it, you're the only one who's not doing anything there, my sister joked the other night on a three-minute transatlantic phone call that hit me like a shot of gin, before triggering a kind of melancholy slump: I'm not not doing anything, I'm adapting, I told her, as her laugh traversed the cosmos, reverberating from one satellite to another before landing in my ear.

And yet, two months ago, when jetlag and panic were keeping me awake on the large mattress we'd plopped on the floor, while the chorus of Sam's and Kid's breathing filled the room, I wasn't so sure I even wanted to activate the spirit of adaptation in me, this decisive aptitude at the root of the survival of the human species. I resisted, bucked, unyielding. The night landing had begun by stealing all landscape, the Denver airport deserted and out of proportion; the police officer at customs had a head shaped like an alembic still, pinkish skin, and empty eyes. He spoke to me in a language in which I had no foothold, in which I could find no protuberance to grasp onto, a language that seemed to have dissolved, melted in on itself. I stammered some inappropriate responses, the officer grew impatient, Kid ended up vomiting the entire contents of a pack of blue Haribo Smurfs gummies, and these had not dissolved, which earned me hostile looks from the people shifting from foot to foot behind me in line, and probably insults as well which I couldn't understand either. I was sweating, ears still blocked from the cabin pressure, and then the corridors went on forever after that, large halls lit up with gigantic ad screens showing the sprawling faces of young women, pupils of their eyes as vast as a heliport, and when we reached the arrivals ramp, I didn't even recognize Sam, who had a beard now and was wearing a hoodie under a leather jacket and jeans that were a little too baggy for someone in their thirties – what happened to you? he asked, eyes shining, kissing me on the forehead and wrapping Kid deep in his jacket.

And then we glided along slow empty highways bathed in cold light, Sam driving a crimson Volvo, an automatic he'd rented for ten days, enough time to find a used one, you have to get your licence, he said, you'll have a hard time without it, and I nodded without conviction. We left the swarm of silvered vertical needles that signaled down-town Denver behind in the continental night and headed due west, towards the Rockies, into the darkness. I kept my nose pressed to the window, Kid fell asleep in the back seat, strapped into a booster seat too big for him – Sam had thought of everything. You okay? He looked at me out of the corner of his eye, then murmured, everything's going to be fine, don't worry, gently caressing my earlobe with his free hand while the American suburb stretched out along the highway as far as the eye could see, dark, reptilian, fanned like embers in a forge – storefront signs, headlight beams, lit windows, phone screens, flashlights, cigarette tips, cat's eyes – I couldn't tear my gaze from this glowing, pulsatile body. This isn't what I expected. What did you expect? whispered Sam, what did you imagine? A dazzling halo hovered in the distance over a horse-shoe-shaped stadium, like a pensive UFO, and fine lines of lights stitched large snail shell shapes far beyond the limit of the suburbs, in the place where new housing projects were being built. I didn't know what to say. I felt like I had landed on another planet.

The night was supernaturally beautiful, the color of blackberries, and whitish smoke from the Coors brewery evaporated into it in large clouds, inverting the light values like a negative photograph. Sam pointed out the muted line of the Rockies through the windshield: we're not too far now. Soon, a wooden arch with yellow letters brought back for fleeting moments a few covers of old *Lucky Luke*s in a teenage bedroom. Sam smiled and exclaimed, eyes dancing: Welcome to Golden – Where the West Lives! This is it? My voice, tight with disappointment, spiraled upward into the high register. He slowed the car and asked me to roll down the window: a current of rural air rushed inside, and with it the dull hum of the brewery like a wind tunnel, and the sound of a river with a corrosive flow. You'll see – in the daytime it's not half bad. We passed slowly beneath the welcome arch as though we were being inducted through a very ancient ritual, and in the light of the streetlamps I made out a few signs with cut-outs of rearing thoroughbreds, cowboys, the stylized ridge of the Rockies, and also the tower of Guggenheim Hall on the Colorado School of Mines campus, where Sam, who'd arrived three weeks earlier, had become a student again for the fall semester. It was almost midnight, the pub was letting its patrons out onto the sidewalk – hubbub of young voices saturated in alcohol – then we drove the last stretch in silence, and I held my breath as we approached the house where we were going to live.

In the day, it wasn't half bad, it's true. The small city flowed like water at the bottom of a canyon between a mesa – a rocky, spectacular formation, with steep sides and a flat top – and the first foothills of the Rockies, a violent and tormented geology that was reminiscent, in paler form, of panoramic traveling shots in westerns, the ones we'd watch on Tuesday nights with the living-room light off to make it feel like the movies, but the black bars that adjusted the aspect ratio to the TV screen had disappeared and suddenly I was there in the picture – because it was, essentially, still that: a picture.

In the early days, I went for a walk with Kid every afternoon, a way to shore up the hours before Sam got home, gradually instituting a ritualized circuit which, over time, allowed the map of Golden – no bigger than a pocket handkerchief – to stick in our brains, Kid's as well as mine. We would leave from Illinois Street in the western part of the city, from the little white house where we lived on the main floor, cross the campus diagonally, and come back up Cheyenne Street before turning onto 14th Street, the neighborhoods wealthier the closer we got to downtown, the canopy of the trees broader and more leafy, the houses older, more elegant, and significantly larger, the gently sloping yards carpeted in emerald-green grass, with slate slabs laid out to create a path up to the front doors. The grass – grown on the rural plain that had been colonized, cleared, subdivided, and made profitable – flowed from the bases of the houses like the green gold of a promised land, perfused the same rich, equitable, and fresh new space. Something in these streets bothered me. The quiet, perhaps – the quiet or the harmony, a partitioning of the community according to an indisputable and silent order: no bark of a dog as we passed, no shout from an argument inside a house to give a glimpse into domestic daily life, like a glove turned inside out, barely the cries of a baby filtered through an open window, the whistle of a pressure cooker, or the roar of a vacuum cleaner. We moved along as though on the squares of a checker board, the perspectives and angles, the distance from one block to the next, the length of the trip, the cadastral logic mixing numbered streets and named ones – a strange mesh in which streets named after Native American nations lay without irony alongside those named after the presidents who had tried to annihilate them – all of this, day after day, became part of us, we gradually got our bearings, walking side by side beneath the tall golden trees, and we too were equal, because we had melted into the same sense of astonishment, the same solitude, and I have never since then had such a dark and violent feeling that we were everything to each other, Kid and I, as during those vacant days, jettisoned but anchored together, and weaving our existence in with that of this place, soon coming to anticipate the make and the color of cars parked in front of garages, betting on the red maple, the pale-blue dog house, the horseshoe-shaped knocker on the black door, a globe in a bay window; we gave names to the houses, to the shapes of people, to the animals and plants, we became familiar, we became neighbors.

Still, every time we turned onto the main street, the high point of the walk, I lost my bearings. I couldn't manage to place where I was, nor even if I was somewhere – the street was unplaceable, I didn't *believe* in it, contrary to Kid who, after dragging his feet through the adjacent streets, came back to life when he saw the shops and bounded ahead like a little goat, always asking for something, a donut, a little car, or that blue stone he'd seen in the mineralogist's window. But something in this part of town toyed with real and fake, as though the main street in Golden was rigged, fabricated for the needs of a story, and as though the welcome arch marked the entrance to a fictional world. In fact, like the small towns of the gold rush that had become ghost towns, Golden had only one street, large and animated, that included a pizzeria, a bike rental place, a hairstylist, a bookshop, and the Rocky Mountains bank branch. Sheds built of painted wood planks stood alongside one or two-story brick buildings, hacienda-style orange stucco buildings, and a whole slew of brightly colored constructions with names done up on the front windows in "western" typeface, all giving the impression of a set, a studio, a picture postcard. And further, at the end of the main street, stood the venerable Colorado School of Mines, founded in the 1870s. Its old campus, its departments of physics, chemistry, and mining engineering dealt, nevertheless, in solid knowledge, in concrete practices, in reliable data capable of describing the materiality of the world and its structure, its resources; this establishment was the first in the world to boast a mining school dug into the side of Mount Zion

– Sam had repeated "in the world" with his finger raised in the air, overplaying the educator as we walked around the buildings the morning after we'd arrived, with me in a daze after a sleepless night and Kid overexcited, shouting, not listening to anything. The school, like the main street, set off the great narrative of origins, recalled the Pike's Peak Gold Rush, the hundred thousand fevered souls who had converged here around 1860, ready to do anything for an ounce of glitter; the school glorified the mining past of Golden – what a name, though – and used this mythical substrate to tell the eternal story of civilization and progress, or how the white man made himself master of the earth and its riches and invented things to exploit its materials, how he imposed his law, how and at what price: force, mud, and Colt 45s, greed, violence: the attempted annihilation of the Indigenous peoples of the Great Plains.

When did I start placing myself in the fable? At first I kept my distance – and maybe a certain mocking grin had even settled into the corners of my lips, the smirk of someone who's not fooled and wants everyone to know it, someone who puts on airs – up until the day when I was at Folks (the renowned main-street store that was also mimicking something, for example the grocery and hardware store of a pioneer town, and smelled like floor wax, onions, and ground coffee) and a woman with her hair braided into a crown hands me a brochure, points to Kid and then up into the air: you should go up there with the little boy! On the ceiling, all I saw was a row of pinkish neon lights. Then I peered closer at the brochure while the woman looked on, probably impatient to see my reaction: Buffalo Bill is buried at the top of the mountain that overlooks the city, the summit of the panoramas, Lookout Mountain, he's right there. I thanked her with a nod, startled: I didn't know Buffalo Bill was a real person and not just a fictional character, a figure of the Far West portrayed some fifty times over in the movies, nor did I know that, in 1882, he'd created *Buffalo Bill's Wild West* show, a history of the "conquest" of the West under the Big Top, which toured in North America and Europe and was seen by more than seventy million spectators – the re-enactment depicted the version of the victors, focusing on the great mythical epic, the moustaches, gold nuggets and guns, using fictional pioneers in Stetsons, but real "Natives," who played out their own attempted genocide while the federal army was massacring them *in real life*.

When we left the store, Kid was glued to my heels, face twisted in frustration, demanding the figurine of an "Indian" on horseback that I'd promised him for another time, you always say that, another time, another time, and then he was refusing to move, shop lights and car headlights were splashing over the street, and I looked up at the mountain, high and dark at this moment, incredibly close, like a body leaning over us, a form that was not human but alive nonetheless, taking us into its arms, holding us, and suddenly, in a twitch of the eyelids, space organized around the red light shining at the summit, as though it was the epicentre, the internal motor, a sort of secret but hyperactive pulse – and similar, now that I think of it, to the red light in church chancels, the gleam I looked for as a child, moving slowly towards the altar, caught in a clever play of shadows and light, in the chromatic shafts from the stained glass, breath shallow, eyelids fluttering but ready to detect, in the triviality of the electric bulb, proof of the true presence of Christ – and standing there in the embrace of the mountain, ultra-fast, a crystallization, I knew I was taking hold of the key to this place, unlocking its design, its occult logic, because now I knew: Buffalo Bill spread his shadow over Golden, watched over the dreams of its inhabitants; he was the guardian figure and the ghost, his spectral presence was part of the mythographic swill that played out here, the blurring of reality. It was getting dark, Kid was tired now, and to distract him, I pointed to the mountain, its black shape against the electric-blue sky, look way up there, do you see the red light? That's Buffalo Bill's tomb! His little face, open-mouthed, turned toward the crests edged with a blood-orange line, and his eyes reflected the first stars while I, as I spoke these words aloud, grew filled with the strange sensation of being complicit in the legend.

It's two in the morning, we're lying on our backs, adrift on a mattress wide as a continent, and with his eyes open in the dark, pupils liquid, Sam asks what it is that disorients me here. Your voice, I answer after a moment of silence. He doesn't react. My voice? Yes. The way I talk, you mean? Not only that – the timbre, the vocal range, all of it. But it's just English, he exhales, it's the fact of speaking a foreign language. I prop myself up on my elbow, facing a crescent moon that sparkles in the night, sharp as a Soviet sickle, and I shake my head: no, your voice has changed.

I don't recognize Sam's voice anymore. Ever since he met us at the airport, when the emotion of seeing each other again, of being reunited for what seemed like a new era in our life together, revived that flushed awkwardness, that mix of momentum and modest pulling back between lovers who've been tested by a separation, I've been able

to make out a variation – one so slight, though, so tenu-
ous that I hardly even paused, because the voice was still
his, there was no doubt, and because we were shaken up
by the situation. But in the days that followed, the impal-
pable shift became clearer, became a seed, tiny, yes, but
it still troubled me. Now, when I hear Sam behind me,
speaking to people who are from here, I sometimes have
to turn around to be sure it's really him talking, because
his voice is progressively converging towards theirs, little
by little toppling over into their community, finding a
way to intertwine with it, to melt into it, as though he was
taking his place within the local orchestra; his voice is
slowly adapting to their tonality, fitting to their rhythm
and volume – Sam speaks significantly louder and slower
here than in France. I watch surreptitiously as he loos-
ens his jaw, relaxes his tongue, spaces out each word and
lowers the roof of his mouth to make the nasal cavities
resonate, all this without thinking, as though he were
following the natural slope of the ground on which he

walks, regulating his voice to make the place his and to belong to it, to make himself heard here. This vocal mimicry doesn't only change his speech, it blurs his whole person: facial muscles I don't recognize have appeared, new attitudes, expressions, and gestures, a way of carrying himself in the world. He doesn't enunciate much now, but enlarges each vowel, his lips moving more than his jaw, his tongue always in the middle. He has shifted his French from the inside, and even when we're alone now, even when he whispers sweet nothings, I can make out the deposits, the traces of these other voices in his, like a continuous echo. The same way a bird changes color to camouflage itself in the branches and fool predators, Sam's voice flows into those of the Midwest, and this disorients me, yes, because it doesn't matter if it's husky, out of breath, disguised by a joke or trembling with emotion, altered by sleep, alcohol, anger, choked with anxiety, or false when approaching someone difficult, this voice has lived inside my ears for so long that one word, barely two syllables, is enough for me to identify it with absolute certainty, to distinguish it from hundreds of others like a track in the mix of the voices that accompany me, to make it out from far away – memory of a radio link in the middle of the night, him in the hull of a small cargo ship in full pitch in the Bering Sea, me lying in the attic of a building on rue Pigalle, the telephone ringing, the receiver brought to my ear with a sleepy hand, hello? static at first, a faraway crackling, and these first vibrations against the membrane of my eardrum that soon touch the three small bones, three crumbs of cartilage, a few milligrams, and grow amplified, converted into electrical impulses that the cochlear nerve transmits to my brain, towards the left superior temporal gyrus, in the place where they've located the microregions of our hearing memory, sensitive to certain speech intonations, to their rhythm and intensity, a sidereal path, the arrow of love, I thought then, sitting up all at once in my bed, wondering about the distance this voice had traveled, carried to me across miles via transoceanic underwater cables and then sent onward by relay antennas standing on the continental shelves, in the middle of plains, at the top of hills, and all the way to the city, the electromagnetic wave invisible but well and truly real, inside my room – this voice is more familiar to me than my own country, it is my landscape. Everyone changes here, you're the only one who doesn't, Sam's voice comes down hard, and then he turns onto his side, his back to me.

I'm sitting behind the wheel of a forest-green Ford Mustang with almond-green leatherette interior. Heavy, lithe, smooth. A racehorse gallops across the grill. The legendary American car. The sound of the engine precedes it, and wherever it goes in the city, people turn their heads to watch it pass – I don't think there are any other Mustangs here, our neighbor Matt had said – he couldn't take his eyes off it – while we stood drinking a beer together on the night of its acquisition.

Sam parked it in front of the house one afternoon in October, ten days after my arrival: I heard a bold rumble, an odd-sounding honk, came out and there he was, leaning against the hood, in chinos and a jacket open over a white T-shirt, arms and legs crossed casually, playing it up. She's from your birth year, he shouted, isn't that wild? Then he turned in profile, feet turned out in dancer's first position, and with a wide gesture of his arm, palm open towards the car, he introduced her like a spellbound dealer: K Coupe, two-door, 271 horsepower, eight cylinders, 4.7-liter engine, three-speed automatic transmission. Steve McQueen's car in *Bullitt,* he concluded with a smile. I stared. How much? Five thousand dollars. Are you kidding? Sam suddenly seemed less solid, more crumbling than I'd thought – the Mustang had no features a couple with a child would need, we would have to contort ourselves to buckle him in, the old seatbelts would jam constantly, the cost of gas would be outrageous, and five thousand dollars was a third of his fellowship. I chased his eyes, which trailed along the body, staying far from mine, falsely captivated by the reflection in the door of the majestic sky. Then he turned towards me like someone who'd acted under duress: we do have to have a car here, you know.

Night was falling, and we headed north toward Boulder. Soon we were rolling into the dusty rose prairie along a road bristling with old electricity poles, while far off the first foothills of the Rockies sketched the backbone of a sleepy stegosaurus who'd escaped extinction. I immediately liked the car's interior, its scent of warm plastic, the alveolar shape that enclosed us together in the same experience, that of our movement, our speed, of an elsewhere that was just there, tangible. Sam was trying to explain to Kid, strapped in the back, that the strength of a horse had become a unit of power used to measure the propulsion of motor vehicles, and that our car was as powerful as a carriage pulled by two hundred and seventy-one horses, but Kid wasn't listening; his head lolled against the back of the seat and he laughed, body shaken, his little pointed teeth gleaming like a wolf pup's – suspension's not great, eh? – and so I was the one struck by this image. When he caught an audible frequency, Sam turned up the radio and a voice came through the

56

static: bluegrass sound, mandolin and guitar, astounding nasalization, ideal, and the voice immediately adapted to the situation like an amplifier, and then the interior took on the dimensions of the outside, the prairie rushed in and the landscape swallowed us all at once – we were a mere mouthful, the three of us. The voice of the singer and the sound of the Mustang aligned, and now they formed a single engine, a single sound unit, which propelled us towards a magnetic horizon line, while another force, this one surreptitious, brought back the images of America we carried inside before coming here, because this country – the States, we'd say in France, pronounced "stets" with the appropriate offhandedness – was familiar to us, we knew it already, we had a picture of it – movies, TV series, ads – and hundreds of Saturday afternoons spent watching, usually sprawled out on a couch in a provincial house, had left a mark. From that moment on a continuum of scenes, landscapes, and faces scrolled past in the back of our brains, subliminal, so much did it

57

seem like we had already been here, that we were back, drifting in a dilated present, such a strange present moment.

The grass had gone blue in the evening shadows, just like Sam's profile, his eyes harpooning the far off, irises backlit by the lights of the dashboard: he was perfecting his attitude, the relaxed fall of his shoulders, the touch of his hands on the wheel, the lightness of his feet that doled out the exact amount of pressure on the pedal when the engine revved high. Watching him from the corner of my eye, I saw that other face I was going to have to get to know, that elsewhere look of those who keep the real at a distance, who slip away, lifting off and gliding into the illusion, those who live out the fantasy, as they say of a life that reverberates movies – here, why not, the road movie about two women on the run headed for the Grand Canyon in a 1966 Thunderbird, emancipated, untethered, sun-kissed, hair in the wind, a string of sumptuous landscapes across the screen, motels, gas stations, and these same electricity poles. Cut the act! Sam burst out laughing. Kid was asleep in the back. Inside the Mustang, we were moving through a secret infra-fiction, gliding through the violet dusk.

Was it because of this, so I could hold something tangible in the palm of my hand, something as unquestionable as a stone, that I started hanging around in front of the mineralogist's window? After fifteen days, when Kid started school, I was gripped by conflicting emotions: the absence of my small companion relieved me of certain daily gestures, released me from the habits that had punctuated our days, but it also removed my bearings, destabilized my rhythm, increased the impression of a blank day, an emptiness, a silence, and I treasured everything I'd had in his presence, his impatience, his desire to run outside, to eat pizza, to go to the pool or watch cartoons over and over on the enormous television we'd bought at a thrift store. At the same time, his absence allowed me a perception of time that was up until then unknown, lavish and exhilarating: "left to my own devices" was the expression, and probably the one that had driven me to the mineralogist, a choice that made a lasting impact on my time in the US, and possibly the course of my life.

The store was called Colorado Magical Stones, but the geographical provenance of the wares on display often exceeded state limits as well as stones, strictly speaking. It had one of Golden's historical signs, one of the oldest on the main street – photographs from 1904 depict its dual nature as a trading post and a cabinet of curiosities. The diorama in the window invariably slowed the steps of passersby discovering it for the first time, and Kid and I had remained transfixed at the window for a long while, our eyes sweeping over the scene: two life-sized wooden mannequins – one representing a person from the Arapaho nation, the other a pioneer, armed and wearing the clothes, hairstyles, and hats of their respective clans – sat trading their finds beside a cardboard fire, feet in the dirt, and among those finds, glinting in their open palms, were flecks of gold and colored stones. I came back later on my own, and the woman with the short grey hair at the back of the store, leaning over some papers and smoking a cigarillo, didn't lift her head when I pushed open the door, setting off an endless electric chime. Small and frail, lips a turned-down red, shoulders narrow, fingers long and twisted as talons, she was wearing round metal glasses and a chambray shirt, the collar pinned closed with an obsidian medallion. I wandered between the Native American drums, the old Colts and daggers, the sheriff stars – some of them suspiciously shiny – the fossils, pottery, and photographs – including the inevitable shots by Edward S. Curtis, and among them some vintage prints worth seven thousand dollars – stuffed deer, bleached antlers, collections of butterflies, engravings of squirrels, tins of spices, ivory dominoes, and I was strangely indifferent to the authenticity of the objects, incapable of discerning fraud, imitation, sham, but intoxicated, excited even; the least curio, the smallest trinket referred to a story, began a tale, called up an image, and

I wove between the aisles through this theater of objects, this immersive kaleidoscope with clouds of tobacco thick as the smoke from a censer, wanting only to believe in this shard of meteorite, this mammoth's tusk, this pipe that Sitting Bull had puffed on for entire evenings, or these arrowheads the size of a fingernail that showed the chromatic variations of the desert – ash rose, monkey's paw, golden rye – labeled "Lithic, or Paleo-American."

I went closer to the wall to see the geology diploma, awarded to Cassandra Fallow by the Colorado School of Mines – cream-colored paper stamped with the black seal and its mining emblems, the pickaxe and the shovel, the gothic font and the name of the graduate in red ink – and then I examined the collection of stones displayed on the dark wood shelves, each with a label indicating its provenance, specifying its components, age, and properties, and I noticed a pebble of an intense bluish green, a crystalline conglomerate speckled with small opaque bulbs, the size and shape of a pear. The woman was checking me out now, cigarillo in the corner of her mouth, her eyes obsidian like the brooch at her throat, and slit, two thin incisions, and then she moved through her paraphernalia to join me, aerial, agile in her thick-soled leather shoes, some ugly and comfortable cross between sneakers and walking shoes, and encouraged me to pick it up, an amazonite from Pikes, Colorado Springs, to hold it up to the light, to weigh it in my hand, touch the stone, feel it, and her voice, aloft on vapors of tobacco, caused the old tumult to be heard.

She used to teach geology at Engineering Hall, and always began by asking each student to consider what lay beneath their feet and to visualize the un-representable: the deep time of subterranean chronology. She had been combing the area for years, exploring it, yes, but also as a scientist and a miner, because she needed to be imaginative – as miners are, she winked – to prospect below the surface of such a territory, and maybe also to go back in time: follow the long-curved wrinkles and fault lines, witness the creation of rivers and the erosion of mountain summits, envision sedimentary layers up to thirty kilometers thick, bring back the Sonoma orogeny and the upheaval of the Rocky Mountains, remember the volcanic eruptions, the storms of ash, the sand dunes covered in clay, shale, or granite, and finally, like an echo from out of time, remember the shallow tropical waters that bathed the area three hundred million years ago, the palpitations of multicellular life stirred in the primitive waves; all of this so as to ferret out stone niches of such quality that once they were torn from the mountain, delivered from their rocky gangue, they went straight to the chests of private collections, the display cases of major museums, the mineral and crystal exchanges of Switzerland, Germany, or China, photographed for the luxury catalogues of prestigious jewelery brands, but the mineralogist kept the most beautiful ones for her own secret stash: she was "mad about stones." I couldn't take my eyes off her, she was speaking quietly and slowly, fragmenting her sentences by breathing time and smoke between each word, creating a duration, stretching out her story, which spread very slowly through the room, filled with something so deep and dreamy I was overcome: all the objects around her were connected, all of them fused together on these scarlet lips that smoked as they talked, talked as they smoked. And so when she told me the exorbitant price of the stone, four hundred and eighty-nine dollars, she emanated a spell so disturbing that I stammered out, I'll think about it, and was getting ready to walk backwards out of the store when she pinched a little shard of amazonite from a bowl full of multicolored pebbles, a rapid movement, and in this moment she was like the bird that plucks a worm from the ground, here, take it – she put it in my hand and closed my fingers around it, and then, while stubbing out her cigarette in the ashtray, her eyes distorted by optical lenses and gazing into mine, she listed the properties of the stone in her gaseous voice: protects from fear, promotes self-expression and autonomy. In that moment I experienced a strange sensation of warmth in my chest, and everything sped up, as though this fragment of matter from the end of time, cored from the Colorado subsoil, was suddenly synchronized to my body, unsheathing its powers, radioactive almost. I could make out the woman's voice from very far off as she advised me now to have the shard made into an amulet, and asked me to come back and see her, because I liked stones too, *I'm Cassandra, what's your name?* I ran home with my fist closed over the amazonite, which seemed to burn hotter and hotter as I ran, and when I opened my fingers at the intersection of Illinois and 16th, I saw, tattooed on my skin, its green star-shaped shadow. *Mad about stones.*

Almost at the pool, where every morning I swim a kilometer: twenty lengths front crawl, ten back crawl, the last ten in a breaststroke – my favorite. My body is changing, visibly – belly flattening, thighs and shoulders firmer. I take South Golden Road and go up Ford Street to 10th, then cross the bridge over Clear Creek – limpid mountain stream turned tumultuous river – glimpse the fly fishermen and multicolored canoes, then the recreation center will appear far off on the left, at the edge of the prairie, an unsuspected combination of sports complex and community center. Its trump card, its centerpiece, is the pool – cathedral ceiling paneled in golden pine and thirty-meter panoramic glass partition wall, swimming lanes and separate baby pool, Jacuzzi, sauna. The first time I went with Kid, who loves playing in the water, and didn't stop laughing, jumping, gulping, until his lips were purple and his eyes red, shivering under a damp towel.

After that I went back alone. Sam, encouraging, would drop me off in the car at the end of the morning circuit, after dropping Kid at school, and then he would head to work, impatient to "start his day" as he'd say – telling me with these words that nothing up until then had really started – but just as anxious about my day, conflicted, hands on the wheel, ready to start the car again, but then he would lean toward me, attentive: you gonna be okay? I'd nod and jump quickly out of the car, closing the door behind me, but sometimes I would stretch the moment out, guileful, and hold him back until he made a face and very lightly revved the motor, shaking his head, sorry, I really have to go now, I have to go – words that I pocketed, deft, before tearing myself away. Then I'd swim three or four lengths to clear my conscience, jamming up the lane where faster swimmers, their heads squashed inside black bathing caps, raced by under the surface like torpedoes and showed their impatience with my seahorse ways, kicking me as they passed, and then I'd go splash around in the Jacuzzi, where my gaze sank deep into the eddies. But soon I felt something racing in my body, something unknown, a phenomenon that was at once irrepressible and overpowering: as the days went by, my swimming time and distance stretched out longer and longer – I discovered a physical endurance, a muscular ardor, and a hunger to use it that I didn't know I had; I stopped floating along, nonchalant, and now I sliced into the surface of the water, throwing my arms far ahead of me like two hoops, regulating my kicking, coordinating my breath, and soon I was swimming without thinking about it, or rather, I was swimming without thinking about anything, and in these monotonous, mind-numbing laps – no doubt I needed to numb my mind – it became clear: I was swimming in troubled waters, I was learning to lose ground.

There are lots of other things to do at the rec center, people go out of their way to tell Sam, well-meaning, and he passes the message along to me before saying, with his eyes elsewhere: you have time for yourself here. A maze of bare and classroom-like rooms holds activities – the multitude made me dizzy at first, and then vaguely repelled: patchwork and scrapbooking, Halloween makeup and Christmas decorations, gingerbread cookies and cinnamon biscuits, country dance, Pilates, drawing, Ping-Pong, squash, and there's also this pottery workshop I caught a glimpse of one night, and I might go, I'm tempted. Bemused, I finally gave in to the idea of mingling with these dynamic housewives who jump out of their Toyota Land Cruisers in colorful leggings and converge here, spending entire days.

You have time for yourself – I still don't know what this means, can barely guess, another reality has burst in, and my life doesn't look anything like itself anymore. Three months ago, I was a young wage-earning urban mother whose life consisted of being late, of walking down the same street to hail taxis that substantially strained my daily earnings, shaking out my bag and my pockets on the landing to find my keys, or racing to the supermarket when it opened to buy the milk that was missing from my child's bowl. I worked for a map publisher, producing the images and adding legends, riveted to a computer screen in an office near Porte de Versailles, frenetic, electrified, caught up in a collective energy, and was proud of my jam-packed calendar. The pool was not for me, and it didn't matter – I only like to swim in the ocean. You have time for yourself.

As for Sam, he gets up early and goes to bed late – halo of the desk lamp on his face at two in the morning as he leans over lined notebooks full of mathematical equations – and only gives himself a few hours off on weekends for a walk, a trip to Boulder, a lunch in Morrison served by two women in flowered cotton apron-style overdresses, like the wives of pioneers of old: those believers with their rye-colored hair and calloused hands. He has joined various research groups, he prepares presentations, gives assignments, meets people, his friends are named Carlos, Haruki, Kurt, Yussef, or Svetlana – above all, he *has* friends, he receives telephone calls and makes plans – we celebrated Halloween at Steve and Pamela's place, a couple in their forties who teach geophysics and play in a metal band, it was snowing that evening, the beer was flowing, and the three of us were dressed up like dogs – while some days, once Kid is at school, I don't speak to anyone all day besides the driver of the shuttle bus, Cassandra the mineralogist, or the girl who makes me a cappuccino on Pine Street. I have become unavailable and solitary. A completely other relationship plays out between me and the world. I think I'm trying to pick up a frequency. And I'm not interested in activities, that's the last thing I want. I don't want anything.

Then I started taking the bus, resolved to figure it out on my own without having to ask Sam to drive me, wanting to take on the territory and certain I could overcome its constraints, its breadth, but also the failures of public transport, a large and distended network in which vast areas, including some that encompassed whole communities – Lakewood, Wheat Ridge, Morrison – remained without bus routes, like waterproof pockets which only the use of cars could render porous. I didn't know then that Golden was one of these, and that in order to get out of this trap, to reach downtown Denver and the Denver Art Museum, fifteen miles from campus, I would have to escape first, to extract myself even, since the shuttle buses – little golden-yellow municipal vehicles – only serviced loops within the city's official limits, never going beyond them. So I looked for a tangential point along their circuit which would get me closer to a stop served by the Denver bus system, and I left at midday, light under a cold sun.

Once I was in the shuttle, I negotiated a stop on South Golden Road, and, being good-natured, the driver agreed – good luck, he called out as I jumped from the vehicle, and I couldn't tell with any certainty whether he was being ironic or, on the contrary, offering a form of tender encouragement, given what I was stubbornly preparing myself to face (and which he had a pretty good picture of himself). In fact, I had to walk three or four kilometers along the noisy four-lane highway on a narrow cement strip meant to serve as a sidewalk. No matter how much I pressed against the bushes coated with dust, the cars still whipped by too close – I felt the air lash my shoulder – some of them honking for a long time, and when they came up alongside me, I caught the hostile gestures of the drivers, mouths deformed by shouts and swearing. I was disturbing traffic, I wasn't where I should be – I was rubbing this place the wrong way. Further along, the bus stop for Denver still hadn't materialized, no posts, no shelters, and I was only able to locate it when I saw a man sitting by the side of the road, silent, eyes masked by sunglasses and Walkman headphones on, wearing jeans stiffened with grime and a parka that reeked of woodsmoke. I stood a little way off to the side from him and, indeed, the bus appeared ten minutes later. Nearly empty.

I sat down at the back on a beat-up seat, pressed my forehead to the window, and suddenly a flow of very white light signaled that something was changing outside, and the recorded voice punctuating the journey announced: Colfax. Blinded, I didn't immediately grasp what was happening along this artery that sliced through downtown Denver for nearly ten miles, and I squinted to see better: parking lots chockablock with cars stretched out on both sides of the bus, as far as the eye could see. Hundreds of dealerships, secondhand car sellers, thousands of cars and pickups, bumper to bumper, coalescing into a single vast metal surface that sparkled in the sun.

Seen from my seat, the rooftops and hoods seemed to have been substituted for the ground so that they formed the body of the plain – the flatness heightened the effect, giving the Denver Basin the appearance of a sparkling lake. Banners and flags floated high in the sky, framing giant signs as solemn and majestic as the flags of countries, their colored logos popping in the monochrome immensity and their letters spelling out the grand alphabet of the American auto industry: Buick, Cadillac, Chevrolet, Chrysler, Dodge, Ford, Jeep, Lincoln, Mercury, Plymouth, Pontiac. And when I saw the galloping horse in the sky, mane blowing in the wind, I remembered that Sam had found the Mustang on Colfax.

The inside of the bus shone like this for half an hour, and no one who got on looked like the people I passed in Golden, on the main street or along the campus paths – no need to be an insider to see it – these folks waited on the side of the road in the wind and were poor and wasted, on foot in falling-apart running shoes: the country wasn't made for them. One – the guy in the parka who smelled like cabin smoke (small damp fire and smoked meat) – suddenly sat down beside me, took off his sunglasses, and with his eyes fixed on my face slowly unlaced one of his shoes, took off his sock, spat in his hand, and started massaging his foot – it was a grey and calloused but powerful-looking foot, the skin streaked with cuts, striated with scars, the nails long and black; a foot with a thick ankle encircled by a barbed-wire tattoo; he pointed it in my direction, put it under my nose so to speak, like a challenge, like a document, while my eyes kept coming back to those tangled lines that fissured the arch, split the callouses, mapped out the state.

Once we reached the first blocks of downtown, the first apartment buildings, and then the skyscrapers, everything turned greyish again, the bus darkened inside, and the next moment it was parking at the base of a glass tower in a lot beaten by winds. Sam and I had noted that the terminus was near the museum, less than two hundred meters from it. How did I do it, then – how did I manage to get lost? Downtown Denver was cold and empty, not one human figure in my field of vision, but a bright stream of cars with tinted windows reflecting the security doors of the buildings. I was going around in circles, disoriented, the good sense of direction I claimed to have – an ace in the hole – had vanished, and I walked, overwhelmed by the gigantic proportions of the official buildings dumbly aligned along inert esplanades, around structures with no doors or windows, but with heavy cupolas and solemn pediments, and when I finally entered the museum, immense, only a few voices resonating near the ticket booths, as in a temple, it was 4:00 and I didn't even have an hour left to see the Indigenous Arts of North America collection, the objects for which I'd made the journey, the reason I had come.

I hurried up the stairs, but as soon as I got to the doorway I knew I would have to slow down: behind the display cases, scattered throughout the room, the works on display inevitably took on the aspect of traces. Partial, worn, fragile, they were presented without staging, in an austere tabulation, a bareness that multiplied their impact. Their materiality hit me in the face: standing before these majestic bison-skin teepees, these cold blankets with graphic embroidery, these tunics decorated with feathers and beads suspended from metal hangers; witnessing these empty wooden cradles painted lovingly in turquoise, or this collar of fur and bear claws displayed on a stand, it was the reality of the murder of so many Indigenous people that became palpable. The objects were so concrete, resistant, irreducible behind the glass wall, they managed to render a presence to a lost world. I stood riveted to the labels that listed the scientific specifications of each artifact: materials, date, location, technique, artist's name. Before leaving, I stood for a long time before an Elizabeth Hickox basket made in 1914, a basket of willow and porcupine quills.

I got my driver's licence. The theoretical test in an agency in Lakewood, and then six hours of in-car lessons, or two afternoons, with a woman named Martina Prewalski who had the particular habit of continuously bringing something to her lips, usually an Oreo cookie, and who used only two words to instruct me: "relax" and "cool." It's easy to get it here, people said, everyone has one. I got mine by performing a basic manoeuver in a deserted parking lot in Wheat Ridge, behind the penitentiary. Done.

The theoretical test itself was over in a quick half-hour, very different from the rite of passage supposed to grant me access to the American expanse, to allow me to go further and to aid in my wanderings. Before starting the engine on the day of the practical test, once I was at the wheel, I took the time to check that my fetish amazonite was still in my jeans pocket, growing warm there in secret, the properties of the stone associated with this driver's licence, this imperative for autonomy that Sam further hardened between us with each new day, arguing that knowing how to drive would make me an independent woman, which I clearly was not, no, you're not, at least not really, he said, and my stubborn insistence on taking the bus or walking had, according to him, no other motive than to show that I was special, to show the people here that I was different, European, educated in real cities, that my home was in a capital city where you didn't have to drive, because the metro system, its arachnidan starring, its lines extending well beyond the ring road, could take you anywhere, and quickly, smoothly; and so not knowing how to drive was a kind of condescension, yes, he nodded, it's a sign of your disdain for contingencies, for practical life, as though I was above all that, but you're not above all that, he repeated, gathering his books and notebooks into a large canvas messenger bag as we reached Engineering Hall, and in fact you're directly concerned by this license thing, because if you drove, your days would be different, they'd be something else entirely, you wouldn't have to wait for me to do your thing, you wouldn't be dependent, you'd be free, and at the last minute, just as he was walking through the door, upset, I called out through clenched teeth, I don't wait for you, I do my thing, I'm not asking you for anything, everything is fine, thank you very much, a scene we seemed to repeat every second day, with its bittersweet variations and raised voices, without managing to camouflage Sam's turmoil, his real worry, the concern he had for me, my acclimatization, because his own stay depended on it: he had made the decision to come and had dragged Kid and me along with him, he had set off the movement, a sudden manoeuver, a twist of fate, but a manoeuver in which I was the secret axis, and which in fact was much more about me than about him, because he couldn't care less about getting a new degree in this dark month of June, he just wanted to go somewhere, somewhere else and far away. He kept trying to divert the grief I felt since the baby that had grown inside me for more than seven months died in my womb, and I was so messed up after the hospital, floating through the two-room apartment on rue de l'Oiseau without even opening the shades anymore, hardly speaking, sleeping nearly all the time, indifferent to other people, neglecting my dear Kid who kept creeping into my bed, licking my cheeks and blowing on my eyelids, what we had been waiting for would never happen, and day after day an unnamed emptiness sucked me up into a dark and icy hole. I had nothing to give but my fatigue, my pathetic body like a vacant husk, and also, I could feel it, this dismay in the face of fatality, in the face of a senseless violence, a dismay that wasn't yet the aloof denial it would become, causing those around me to fall silent, and Sam's loving gestures were the only ones I would accept, we're getting out of here, he'd say over and over, we'll leave behind everything that wounds, that aches – he held my face in his hands and spoke against my forehead – we were going to change course, the Colorado School of Mines was a perfect excuse, and Sam was ready to use all the fables to pull me out of the slump I was in, including telling himself a completely different story, ready to leave three weeks earlier than us to scout it out, to sleep in a motel on Colfax where he worried the polyester sheets might go up in flames, where the voices of TV announcers – the American soundtrack: commercials, pornographic heavy breathing, news – the sound of taps and the flush of toilets, telephone conversations, fights, all of it came through the walls of his room no thicker than cigarette paper; ready to redo high-level math with a bunch of twenty-year-olds, and above all ready to believe – but for all this to work, I had to do my part, goddamn it, and for that, I had to learn to drive.

On the first day, Martina was waiting for me in front of the house at the appointed hour, leaning against the door of a metallic-grey Honda Civic, which, when I saw the pile

of clothes, dirty sneakers, and disemboweled Oreo pack-
ages on the back seat, I understood to be both her work
tool and personal vehicle. She held out a cool, plump
hand, looking me up and down from the depths of her
small, deep-set grey eyes, and invited me to get in with
a casual motion of her hand. After a basic presentation
of the dashboard, pedals, and gear stick, we set off down
6th Street West, all the way to Colfax. Traffic was moving
well, and Martina described every one of her actions, her
least movements, insisting on the importance of breathing – she took one hand off the wheel and placed it on
her large, round belly – and repeating, over and over,
the steps required to pass someone, turn, or change
lanes, in a low, monotonous, and vaguely syrupy voice,
her words emerging in a perfectly rhythmic flow, a regular pattern in which each stressed syllable offered her
a sort of place to rest, the possibility of setting off again,
and, I could hear, something to talk about continually for
hours – one, I look in the rearview mirror; two, I turn on

my indicator; three, I turn the wheel; four, I accelerate with the right pedal to overtake; and five, I shift down a gear. The inside of the car was saturated with instructions, like a temple full of mantras, and I listened, eyes on her doll-like profile, her curls as tight as a ribbon around a present, snub nose, full cheeks, frosted lips, and a chin that jiggled slightly whenever she turned her head a bit sharply, which didn't happen often because she was a calm person, in a large pink sweatsuit made of thick and comfortable fleece, with a rhinestone feather embroidered on the belly.

After a while, Martina told me not to stare at her like that and to look, instead, at her hands, her shoulders, her legs, her eyes: your entire body is involved when you're at the wheel – and I watched hers for a moment before turning back to face the road, her voice in my ear rocking me so gently I could have driven all the way to the ocean, and then, after an hour, she slipped a different phrase into her monotonous threnody, a few words like a bit of grit in my ear, I've got to go home, and immediately after that we turned south towards Aurora, in the suburbs of Denver, which did not fit its name, since nothing dawned here, especially not light – the least spark had been outlawed in these parts, and the dullness had nothing to do with how dirty the windshield was and everything to do with the urban phenomenon that seemed to exhale in these parts, out of breath, crawling, reduced to a horizontal thrust, an endless grid of bare, transparent, almost diaphanous streets. The absence of trees, the single-story buildings, the flat roofs, all of this gave an impression of being crushed, of the ground cowering – something in Aurora dragged low, flattened in the dust of the plain, in the sorrow of the earth. Martina drove slowly, reciting her instructions at every stop – one, I turn on my indicator; two, I stop the car; three, I look both ways; four, I accelerate – and soon we had entered a place called Meadows Park, which further radicalized the partition of the ground, the land divided into lots, then parcels circumscribed in chalk where prefabricated homes had been delivered by truck on narrow flatbed trailers, houses without foundations or even a crawl space under the floor, more or less identical to those, spindly, makeshift, that we imagine flying into the air, pulverized, blown to smithereens in the eye of the first tornado. She parked three driveways down in front of a pale-yellow mobile home with aluminum siding, surrounded by a rectangle of dirt and gravel that yesterday's storm had transformed into mud, this is my place here, got out of the car saying she wouldn't be long, and I watched her disappear behind the scrawny partition into an invisible off-camera where I guessed, from seeing the porch and the toys abandoned in the muck, there lived at least one child. It was three o'clock, the sky was flat, the color of sick barley, and the silence, now, comparable to the continuous hum of a refrigerator, a silence so strange, so all-consuming I couldn't even distinguish it from myself, as though it came from inside my brain, mixed in with the pulsations of my blood, and not from this trailer park where even though the mobile homes housed hundreds of human lives, still an impression of nothingness caulked the place, not a living soul, I thought, a little too quickly, because it was less an emptiness than an excess, too much presence that seeped – aphasic, stifled presences, oppressed by poverty, a net curtain that lifts behind a dirty pane, a child who steps half naked onto the doorstep of her trailer with a can of beer in hand and gives me the finger, two guys bumming around on the corner over there, and furtive, feral cats. Since the wait was stretching on – even the idea of waiting, here, was absurd, in this trailer park where no one had been waiting for anything for a long time, unless it was for life to go on as it had, keeping misery on par with the pavement and no lower, please, not worse than that, because they still had to gather up the three hundred and fifty dollars a month to rent the parcel of land, and added to that the rent for the trailer itself, all of which could rack up to seven, eight hundred a month, and this just to have the right to stop somewhere, to breathe – since Martina wasn't reappearing, I looked around the inside of the car and ended up opening the glove compartment, looking for a guide book, or better yet a topological map, something to read, to look at, and as I groped around in the cavity I felt something cold and hard that I picked up and drew out into the light of day, not that shocked, really, beneath this dirty sky, beside these scraggy walls, these poorly mounted windows that let a bitter wind blow through, to be holding a gun in my hand. A handgun, they say, a black pistol with a metal butt and short barrel, and I hefted it in my palm, looking at it from all angles, trying to identify the mechanism in the thing, vaguely remembering words like "barrel," "lock," and "trigger," words that floated above a diagram without actually landing on any particular part of the object, unable to caption it, then, but resorbed into this single syllable, "gun," explosive, all in the mouth, packed, aggressive, and, well, it was the first time I'd seen one in real life, the first time I'd held one in my hand – up until then I had only known Granny's rifle, the one we'd take into the field behind the house to shoot at wooden targets and break up the heatwave boredom of July in Charente – and more than the idea of death crouching in the back of the barrel, it was the compactness of the object that troubled me, its enigmatic density; and, hypnotized, I didn't hear Martina come out of her place, pass through the little fence, useless as wire mesh, that sectioned off her parcel, and it was only when she heaved two huge plastic bags into the back of the car and slammed the door that I jumped, panicked, unable to gauge the time needed to put the gun back in its place before she got into the car, hesitating for a fraction of a second, another lapse that was too long, because when Martina heaved herself into the driver's seat, I had only enough time to shove the glove compartment closed with my knee and slide the gun under me – under my right buttock to be precise, on the door side. Martina tossed me a smile before starting the car, let's go, and started up her litany again, contenting herself with counting, now, stopping after uttering the number so that I would finish her sentence, so I would complete it, filling in the right action, the right move to make, which I did with some difficulty, having trouble remembering, stammering, and disturbed to feel, under my ischium, Martina's gun, which may have been low-profile but still had a thickness to it, and it left me unbalanced, my back twisted, left shoulder perceptibly lower than the right, a difference I compensated for by stretching my spine up straight – the situation was completely beyond me, it projected me into another dimension of reality, a hyper-concrete dimension, because the pistol under me was not an image, it was hard as a stone, and it hurt. We took the highway in the opposite direction, driving toward the Rockies which I had never seen towering so tall over the plain, stretching across the windshield like a monstrous wave, the sixty-meter-high kind you see on the horizon in Nazaré,

Portugal, and suddenly Martina interrupted her mantra and told me we were going to make a quick stop to drop off her laundry – she motioned with her chin toward the bursting bags on the back seat, glanced at her watch, and repeated, a quick stop. I immediately envisioned the movements I'd have to make to put the gun back into the glovebox as soon as her back was turned.

When we turned right toward the mesa, Martina yawned several times and I glimpsed, along her top jawline, a large hole where the first two molars on the right should be. Sorry. She had been working late, she was ironing for some people in North Table Mountain, she took both hands off the wheel to make the shape of an enormous cone because it was a huge mountain of laundry for a large family, then said, I need cash. Her voice changed, syllables choppy, vowels turned heavy and rough, as though scraped from the back of her throat and expelled with anger, a staccato output very different from the monotonous and languid flow she'd uttered on the way to Aurora. I need cash. There you have it. She wanted to get out of Meadows Park, too much crime there, too much violence, terrible reputation, you never find work when people know you live there, and I have two sons who will never be trailer trash, I'm telling you, there's no way, and with that, she cocked her indicator and sped up to overtake a tanker going slow as a snail, the father of her kids had split, vanished, poof – her fingers fluttered above the steering wheel, a flight of butterflies – and her salary at the driving school wasn't enough to cover the loans, she wanted to go back to Lakewood and she seized every opportunity, mowed the grass for a Korean professor down by the campus and worked on Sundays in a retirement home – she let out a little laugh as she said the name of the place: Fossil Trace Center! – she had invested in a steam iron she hoped to have paid off by the end of the month, and by the way – her voice suddenly slowed, stretching out the final syllables like bubble gum – by the way, if you wanted, I could take care of your laundry, it

95

would be no problem, she had misinterpreted my painful grimace and told me that the woman we were going to see had been her student, she had taught her how to drive, I could have complete confidence.

The highway interchange in the shape of a giant fly had spit us out at a stretch of scrawny bushes, and very quickly another subdivision appeared, with large houses, these ones solidly built: two garages, three storys, four slopes to the roof. Here we are. She slowed in front of a light-colored house from which a large blond woman wearing a heather-grey sweatsuit emerged, followed by a well-built boy carrying two more bags of laundry, and without a word he made the exchange for the bags on the back seat. The woman knocked on the window, then handed Martina a thin wad of cash and asked her to be back at the same time tomorrow, punctuating the trans-action with a wink that deepened her crow's feet, please, Martina, come on. Martina turned toward the bags in the back, even bigger than the last ones, and seemed to hold back her answer, pinching her lips to stifle a sigh – if I say no, she won't ask me anymore, I have to do it, this is what she said to herself – and with an exhale, she nodded, stiff curls bobbing on either side of her cheeks, okay. We did a U-turn, heading back towards Golden. Martina came back to life and bit into a cookie, starting up the chant of her lesson again, voice softer now, but the thing I was sitting on took up all the room in my brain and I didn't say anything more, dazed by this scene settling in me: Martina, unstable, anxious, exhausted, racking up jobs in her Honda – and in the process charging, at least I hoped, hours, gas, and kilometers to the driving school – and me contorted in the passenger seat, hatching a revolver.

You're going to drive the last few miles, she announced, pulling over on the side of the road that ran west along Cherry Creek all the way to the upper part of campus, you must be impatient to drive, right? I stammered that I didn't know, playing for time, realizing I would have to get up to exchange places with her, and in so doing would reveal the gun, what do you mean you don't know? Her brow was so prominent it created a kind of visor above her zinc-colored eyes, and I clung to her voice, indisputably authoritative in this moment. What don't you know? Of course you're going to drive, you have to, you're going to drive yourself home, sugar, think of your husband, of your little boy. I was paralyzed. I finally opened the door, slowly, a signal that set off the same movement on Martina's side, and as she extricated herself from her seat, turning her back to me, leaving the motor running, I made a move – with what? my hip? – to make the pistol slide onto the floor of the Civic, but instead it fell into my bag which was sitting open at my feet. Martina and I passed each other in front of the hood, she gave me a little pat on the back, relax, and the next minute I was rolling towards Illinois Street, panicked and exhilarated, unable to stabilize my speed, the car moving in spurts along a path that was not exactly straight, oscillating on the road like a stiff, strange body, and moreover seeming vaguely opposed to my authority, indifferent to the inflections of my will, a body that may well have been aligned with my own by the play of an elementary mechanics and was in some sense an extension of my person, but was nevertheless still unknown to me, like a rebellious transplant, a substance that (I was only too aware in each vibration undulating over my skin, in each contraction of my muscle fibers) had its own life, an excessive life, a life that wanted nothing more than to escape me, and that did – it escaped me. I was going at a snail's pace, trying to calm the situation by not making any particular intention manifest, forcing myself not to think about the gun in my bag, reciting in an automatic voice each of the steps required to slow down, turn, overtake, change lanes, stop, Martina's sentences echoing, sonorous and well-articulated in my mouth, and since she was egging me on, I had the vague impression that we were singing together.

I slowed in front of my house and saw Kid's little head

pop up at the window as Martina clapped, very good, you're doing well, then said she'd see me tomorrow, same time same place, and I picked up my bag and closed the door behind me. Once I was out of the car, I watched the rear lights until they disappeared: would Martina head towards Meadows Park to start ironing the huge mountain of laundry for the large family, would she go mow the lawn of the Korean professor near campus, or was she headed to pick up another student to teach them how to be independent? I climbed the steps, in a hurry to be home, and just as I stepped through the door the image of Martina's smile came back, a smile so big that the gap in her molars suddenly reappeared.

The apartment looked like a quiet, warm, and cozy home on a winter's night, and when I opened the inside door, my steps loose, bag a little heavy in the crook of my elbow, Kid rushed toward me followed by Sam, smiling, tender, and mocking – so? I almost wanted him to rifle through my bag so he would discover the gun – like a bit of customs loot – and think through this unlikely situation with me, because I had managed – but how the heck do you do that? – to find myself weighed down by a firearm, to bring into my house the very object of my fears, but Kid was whirling around us, and the minute I stopped watching him he took my jaw in both hands to turn it back sharply towards him, talking to me ten centimeters from my face, and so I ended up plonking him down in front of a cartoon and motioning to Sam to come with me into the basement, a place I never went, where I had only been once or twice since we got here because I was scared of it – I associated these seeping rooms lit by a bare bulb with crimes, with the hundreds of millions of firearms that circulated in this country, with serial killers and mass shootings, the guy who draws his automatic rifle in the doorway of the McDonald's and guns down twenty people before blowing his own brains out – and I would laugh at my terror, I'd joke about it but never to the point of being able to go down the stairs and casually start the washing machine, you're the one who's seen too many movies, Sam would say, shaking his head, exasperated, and he'd lug the little mountain of laundry for his little family himself, and now he must have thought I was taking him to the basement for a sultry ambush because he was suddenly there, playing innocent, his voice concerned, what is it? I stood under the cold light, opened my bag and took out the gun, slowly, and instead of collapsing in astonishment, he trembled and whispered: what is that thing? We examined the object together and watched it reflect this country we had come to, while I told him quietly and at top speed about my first driving lesson, a lesson in which I had ended up doing something completely different than learning to drive, but which had driven me elsewhere, here, to the place I didn't go, the place I never would have gone, while Sam stolidly kept me going with simple technical questions – Do you have her number? When is your next lesson? – questions that managed to deactivate the pressure on the gun, its fetishistic aura, hot potato of violence, and made it seem instead like an accessory in the American arsenal, a gun made of plastic, and then Kid appeared on the stairs, a little wisp of a thing in his grizzly-bear pyjamas: someone's here. We took the stairs two at a time and when we got to the kitchen, there was Martina, stolid herself and smiling, traces of chocolate at the corners of her mouth, her hand outstretched: give it back.

Rides in the Mustang have become a daily thing, setting off when the afternoon grows wider, when the light whitened and everything around me seemed suspended from this action: grabbing the car keys in a single swift gesture and then off we go. In the beginning, I looked for an excuse, a simple errand – a lined notebook with a soft cover, a black pen with a fine point, a novel, a newspaper in French, film for the camera, stamps and envelopes – to justify these car trips of several hours that took me far, far beyond the limits of my familiar perimeter, and only finished at the end of the day in front of the doors of the Davy Crockett school. But little by little I let go of the excuses, points around which my trips unfolded more or less consciously, and I just left, with no other aim than to drive, giving myself over to the surface, to the urban flow, immersive, arbitrary. I would sit down behind the wheel and take the time to adjust the chair back, the distance from the pedals, then start the car, and soon I'd be rolling at a slow and steady speed, a cruising speed, sending myself out at random, decentered, disoriented, multiplying the variations, deviations, diversions, and perspectives. Often once I had set out, I would turn on the radio, and immediately be stalked by a religious sermon on one channel or another, reeled off in a masculine voice with perverse modulations, by turns seductive and threatening, cavernous, and I would steer clear of these, choosing music instead, a melody, a song I could sing loud and clear, at the top of my lungs, as they say – it feels so good to sing loud, shaking your head; and if I turned down the volume I could hear my own voice, hesitant but incredibly distinct, it would come back to me and insist, as though these hours alone in the car were made for this and this only: to hear myself. These hours, which were neither aimless wandering nor even an exploration, stretched out in the form of excited anticipation, an open game, in which the monotony of the suburb, its infinite continuity, but also the trips to the hills, to the rocky folds of the mountain, could at any moment bring back an image, a thought, a voice, and connect in me the parts that stood disjointed.

I ended up getting lost – all this was made for it. One muddy afternoon, as I wove along the slopes of greyish grass above Golden where identical houses are grouped like bones at the bottom of a bag, the road suddenly disappeared: past the hood, a gravel path extended out between black pines. A wooden sign with a pictogram signaled the entrance to Triceratops Trailhead, the hiking trail at the edge of campus. I immediately thought of Dino, whose plastic eyes with vinyl lashes meet mine, and then, as though the Mustang were a magical chamber, the interior dissolved all at once and Kid appeared before Cassandra the mineralogist, the day she told him in halting French: this is dinosaur territory. He was standing with a tuft of hair sticking up at the top of his head, shy but intrigued. Around them, the objects in the store seemed to silently acquiesce, and I leaned in. Dinosaurs have been dead a long time, there's not a single one left on earth, he answered, unflappable, and Cassandra nodded and said in a drawl, yes, you're right, then went to get a cardboard box from a shelf and unwrapped something brownish the size of an adult man's thumb, I couldn't tell what it was made of – stone, resin, petrified wood, plastic? Look, she said to Kid, a dinosaur tooth. And then she lit a cigarillo: Colorado has one of the largest deposits of dinosaur fossils in the world, a boy like you must know that. In the car, now, I saw Kid again as he went closer, peering at the object with its orange tag – $100 – and then turned towards me: is it real? I picked it up and it shone, polished, the point blunted; I imagined it as an incisor in the jaw of a timid diplodocus, busy grazing on tree ferns at the river's edge, and I decided it was real. And then I steered him toward the illustrated books and bought a comic about the disappearance of the dinosaurs, a giant-sized book that Kid opened right away, flopping to his knees in the middle of the store.

The rain drummed on the hood of the Mustang, streamed down the windows, obscuring the landscape, the outside vanished, while the images of this comic book – a real classic, said Cassandra – were outlined clear as day. Because the truth is, Kid and I lived inside this book with its fascinating illustrations for a time. The paleo-artists and illustrators didn't skimp on any details to impress us: dinosaurs stood across a full-page spread, immediately mythic, most of them terrifying, pictured in an interlacing of scholarly notations and fantastical scenes, the earth not yet populated by humans, of course, but the dinosaurs all mixed together on the same plate, whether or not they truly co-existed – a carnivorous *Tyrannosaurus rex* with red eyes bit into a diplodocus who lived sixty million years before it. Every night we went over the hypotheses that explained the dinosaurs' extinction, and though Kid liked the most spectacular of them, the Big Bang, the impact of an asteroid sixty-six million years ago, though he reveled in its cataclysmic impact, the earthquakes, tsunamis, and hurricanes it caused, though he was passionate about the idea that a cloud of particles released during the shock had plunged the planet into darkness and caused a fatal nuclear winter, I was drawn to another theory, an ambiguous and tragic one, the theory of an evolutionary dead end, the senescence of the species during the Cretaceous period when dinosaurs, suffering from gigantism and suddenly endowed with these absurd anatomical structures, became heavy and slow, unable to rival the other creatures – their heads bobbed up and down shaking their vain ruffs, bent under the weight of aberrant horns, melancholy has-beens – and finally collapsed on the riverbed, swept along with the rocks. When Sam showed up at nightfall, he found us stretched out on the floor inside the big open book, Kid hugging Dino and me with my cheek against his neck, nose right up in the pictures, anxious at the thought that species which don't adapt will invariably disappear.

The rain had stopped, the car dripped, the forest streamed, and everything outside was changed. I started the engine again. Triceratops Trailhead went a few meters and then disappeared into an area where paleontologists had unearthed fossils and imprints. Kid, of course, wondered if these creatures might one day come back to earth, and if it would be possible to spend time with them peacefully, to make them into allies, and why not even friends? Watching *E.T.* one Sunday afternoon, the three of us cuddled together, he held his breath, captivated by Elliott's encounter with this little intergalactic dinosaur who gets lost in an American suburb much like the one where we lived. Kid was enchanted by the extraterrestrial's incredible kindness but revolted by the cruel stupidity of the adults and started to cry; Sam gently stroked his arm, and then I burst into tears too at the moment when the creature's long greenish finger pointed out the starry sky and, in his inimitable voice, he asked if he could phone home. He's homesick, Sam whispered, his slow eyes looking into mine, and he spoke the word "homesick" the way you'd throw a hook. I'm not homesick, I would have liked to say, as Elliott lifted off and soared across the yellow moon – enormous in the Hollywood sky – with a dinosaur in his bike basket, it's just that the things I'm living through here have rendered everything I once thought I knew unrecognizable.

The landscape tilts, the sky moves over the jagged crest of the Rockies, pours from west to east and swells above the plain, filling up all the space. The back of the Safeway appears on my left, the long wall of orangey brick visible between trees – "safe way," the secure path, carts piled high with salt-and-vinegar chips and graded apples, perky salespeople saying, "how are you today?" fluorescent-green peas and bluish milk, pop songs playing from speakers above aisles strewn with sawdust, Christmas decorations up immediately after Halloween pumpkins; "safe way," the peaceful route, controlled. The gas station is on the other side of the parking lot and that's where I'm headed to fill up.

Sam and I spoke this morning of the future of the Mustang, and the idea of bringing it back in a month – sending it across the Atlantic in a cargo ship a month from now to use over there – was quickly squelched: prohibitive cost, high fuel consumption, but above all, a car that would be incongruous at home, noisy, dissonant even, out of place. We'll sell it before we go back. Sam got up, rubbed his hands together and said, okay, it's settled, we won't speak of it again. Then: it will be a memory. His face, turned towards the window, was bathed in morning light, and any bitterness was undetectable. It will be a memory.

I slow at the intersection, put on my indicator to turn left, stop, a Dodge and a red pickup go past, and I wait, I have all the time in the world. I think again of Kid, who mumbled something in English yesterday, concentrating, bathtub full of multicolored plastic figurines, tiny cowboys spiraling in the water, and when the way is clear, I press on the accelerator, the motor responds, and I turn onto the drive that leads to the Safeway. It is so simple, so easy, and traffic is so quiet at this time, no congestion, not a single obstacle, nothing that could disturb my field of vision – but maybe I am too sure of myself in that moment, or maybe I am elsewhere, contained inside my solitude where something fragile is growing at this very moment, something that belongs only to me and that I protect the way you protect a secret – and I must have misjudged the pressure of my foot on the pedal and cranked the wheel too hard, because the Mustang jumps, a jolt, my head falls forward and then snaps back, my body clenches and hands cramp. I can't manage to right my course and end up drifting left into the opposite lane, cutting off the unsuspecting cars driving in the opposite direction – it is the first Tuesday in December, an ordinary day in the middle of the 1990s, it is starting to snow out there at the base of the hills, the first flakes fall slowly on the great prairie which the white men had attempted to scour of Plains Peoples, this prairie where smoke billows from the brewery making American beer, the same prairie Martina criss-crosses in her Honda, tough, a revolver in her glove compartment and bags of wrinkled laundry in the back seat. Boom! A dull soft sound inside the car. I have hit the front of a caramel-colored Buick, which is knocked off its axle in a long honk of the horn, a groan, and in this ultra-quick second I glimpse, like a still from a movie, the stunned long pale face of the professor of microeconomics from Sam's department, an austere and angry guy, and then my feet go haywire, I jam the brake pedal down, I have to brake, I have to at all costs pull over on the side of the road and face the economist in his Buick, but instead the opposite happens, I speed up, everything goes very fast, the road is going very fast, the car pitches down an embankment, rolls over in the grass, the noise inside the vehicle changes and then is suddenly stifled, I am shaken, reality rushes forward, it is out of control, and then I soar.

The Mustang nosedives and I can feel that I have toppled, too. The shock wave continues to thicken space – it completes the accident. Stamped sheet metal in slow motion, the material warped forever. Silence slams into the car. Something irreversible has happened.

The voice of a man, far off: are you okay? The sound of knocks on the door. I take a breath, I'm safe. I open my eyes, move an arm. Don't move! The parking lot is below, the Mustang is balanced on top of two vehicles parked side by side, two cars that didn't ask for this. The cops are already here, four or five of them, and in their midst, the sheriff with his star – this is not a dream – he steps past the others in his boots with pointed toes, bulging inside a leather coat, aghast, lifts his head toward me and asks in a louder tone: who are you? I shift in the seat and the Mustang shifts too. Voices ring out below, don't! don't! I manage to open the door, which detaches from the body all at once in a clatter of metal and hangs in the void. A cop comes closer and holds out his arms so I can climb down – just the same as if I were dismounting a horse – catching me around the waist and setting me down on the ground. All right, young lady? I find my footing in the midst of the flashing lights and sirens, in the midst of these American voices that sound like the ones you'd hear over walkie-talkies in the eighties. A movie stunt. I take a few steps in the parking lot. People make way for me, watching me like a strange animal – I'm the green mouse from the song. I can't talk, my jaw is locked. Witnesses are already miming the scene to the stunned police officers, making big gestures in the sky, I can hear them yelling: out of control, crash, this woman must be crazy. No one understands anything. I have to tell Sam.

As news of the accident spreads, people come running over to the Mustang and stand with their arms crossed over their chests, elbowing each other, screwing up their faces, a fucking beautiful car; and some give me the stink eye. People pushing their carts out of the Safeway stop short, their stupid eyes wide, hands over their mouths, oh my gosh, and some wait to see what'll happen next. A woman, her cart overflowing with provisions, is talking to a police officer who points to me, and she turns her head, our eyes meet – one of the two cars under mine is hers. A man opens the back door of an ambulance and pulls a stretcher over to me, but no, no, it's okay, I'm okay, unscathed, not a scratch, not even a bruise – had my face been covered in blood, things would have been different, my shame and embarrassment would have been less. The cold envelops me. I wish I could just disappear like the species that didn't adapt.

It will be a memory – this phrase comes back to me, circular and predictive, as I watch the tow truck's pliers prepare to lift the Mustang by the roof. And then I see Sam, running straight toward me through the parking lot, slaloming between vehicles, bystanders, and carts, his trajectory indifferent to all that's flashing and red, to those who call out, sorry man, and to the delicate operation happening just a few meters away, the car wrecked, unrecognizable, suspended in the air. He's here, out of breath, and takes me in his arms without a word, pulls me inside his jacket and holds me for a long time, stroking my head, and I burst into tears against his sweater while he murmurs: you sure made a hell of a mess. Then he lifts his head, turns to see, and little by little his face is distorted by retroactive fear, the disconnect between the state of the car and my intact body. One sec, I'll be right back.

I'm lying in the grass, arms outstretched, eyes on the sky. They're going to question me soon, I'll have to gather up the facts, describe what happened, tell the story. It's snowing now, huge flakes hovering silently in the air, the least breath causes them to swirl, the first ones so fragile, so delicate, they evaporate the second they touch the pavement. Soon they'll cover everything. I remember that Dino is still in the Mustang, as well as the small box holding a bowl I made here out of clay. The pottery class happened at night, and in the end I went: I liked going out in the evening while Sam and Kid were building bridges out of Kapla blocks on the living-room carpet, and driving in the dark, hearing the river from the rec center parking lot, the quiet in the studio, the scent of earth and water, concentrating, trying, failing, and holding the dream of one day making a bowl, a simple bowl, in which I could keep what I had gathered up here, and bring it home.

# Nevermore

I CLOSE one soundproof door after another behind me and step into the studio, blinded by the rays of light: the mic, a Neumann U 87 Ai Condenser, sits in the sling of a metal suspension shock mount, awaiting me – perched on a tripod like a king cobra.

Fibrous half-dark, black ceiling perforated with spotlights, walls lined with soundproofing foam, nubbly, and alveolar, the booth is like a cockpit: office chair, black melamine table, small lamp pointed at printed sheets of paper, and this completely unmoving glass of water – a Dutch still life. In this basement apartment, where the low acoustic pressure creates an atmosphere of interiority at once dull and profound, I immediately feel I am assembling a center – my own – and I take possession of the place, stretching out time, play-acting the professional I might yet become. I sit at the table as though I am the final piece of a three-dimensional puzzle, place my two feet flat on the ground and pull my hair back into a ponytail before putting on the headset, then push up the sleeves of my sweater – the small knobs of my wrist gleam like marble knucklebones. Next, I warm up my voice like a star of the Conservatory: quick vocal exercises up and down the scale; movements to dispel micro-tension around the jaw, trills, $b$'s and $p$'s to relax the lips and tongue – I discipline the least agitation in my body, establish calm like royalty. I'm ready.

On the other side of the glass wall, the Klang sisters stub out their cigarettes, standing before the console. Then I hear a voice in my headphones, casual: say something, we're checking the levels, the first stanza of the poem for example. I set the text down on the table in front of me and start to read: *Once upon a midnight dreary, while I pondered, weak and weary, / Over many a quaint and curious volume of forgotten lore – / While I nodded, nearly napping,* I cast a glance towards the control room where one of the sisters, perched on a stool, traces little circles in the air with her index finger, circles that mean keep going, keep going, so I go on, *suddenly there came a tapping, / As of someone gently rapping, rapping at my chamber door. / "'Tis some visitor," I muttered, "tapping at my chamber door – / Only this and nothing more."* Great, thanks. Leaning over sheets of paper criss-crossed with ballpoint pen, the two of them are speaking quietly to each other now, so close, so attentive to each other that the words "to join forces" seem to have been created expressly for them – and they are physically similar as well, both ageless, long and thin, in flannel trousers and white sneakers, with gunmetal manes of hair, one sister with a Giants cap and the other with a small orange Rhodia notebook around her neck like a doctor with her stethoscope. The Klang sisters. Inge and Sylvia.

Ten days ago, the crystalline tinkling of a text had confirmed this session, and I stopped in front of the Conservatory in the middle of rue Blanche before accepting a proposition I knew wouldn't earn me a dime: the recording would not be remunerated, and the broadcast rights would be handled in a letter of agreement I imagined to be scalpel-hewn. But the Klang sisters, wow, that's something! Legendary pair, cult catalogue. A monumental work that aimed to restore to literature its oral aspect, to embody it, to give each text a voice all its own, the right one – they never recorded more than once with the same person – we're interested in the voice, they informed people, haughty, but above all we're interested in the listening it creates, and they rubbed their fingertips together gently beside their ears.

They pan for voices like gold in the river, without faith or law, throw themselves into the depths of crowds, organize once-a-month auditions on a Sunday that have become mythic, attracting post-synchro professionals and students from the Conservatory; and when April arrives, they leave for their "great collecting," spending several weeks aboard a VW bus-cum-recording studio which takes them to the front steps of high schools, behind abattoirs, into courtrooms, and onto the stages of theaters, along beaches and through markets, to the edges of stadiums and hospitals, to the heart of ports and churches – and they remain on the alert even in the changing rooms of municipal pools where they swim their daily kilometer, head to toe in the same lane. It's said they understand each other instantaneously and that, when they overhear a desirable voice, they scheme to record it on the spot, leading the person into the little bus, polite but rapacious, and you should see the face of the chosen one then: dumbstruck, imagining a prank, a hidden camera, suspicious as they climb inside – and then emerging again an hour later brandishing a copy of the recording on a flash drive as their prize – a Laforgue poem, the technical manual for a Dyson, or Obama's inaugural address. We'll call you – and sometimes, indeed, they do.

When they get back to their house studio in the 14th arrondissement, they say the Klang sisters listen to their recordings through headphones for days on end. The voices infuse them as, simultaneously, the sisters cover the books they love with notes, then enter the tessitura into a database using keywords that sometimes pile up, the list of which would unhorse the best agents of the British cipher – vocables along the lines, perhaps, of: "décolletage," "revolution," "myopic," or "cigarillo." Next, collected in this extraordinary vocal color chart, the voices metamorphose: soon they have no gender or age – although the Klang sisters are wary of children's voices – and instead of being the voices of professions or knowledge, or even social or geographical voices, they become pure acoustic material. They are low or high, bright or gloomy, glottal or clear, gritty or sibilant, marmoreal or porous, airy, guttural, nasal, they are husky, broken, deep, or bewitching, they are lively, fluting, far off.

My voice, heard for the first time while the Klangs prowled at dawn between the chestnut trees in front of the Conservatory, and later tagged as "light canoe on dark ocean," was thus correlated to my cell number on Sylvia's little Rhodia notepad. Inge had me read an article she pulled out of her bag about the reform of the common agricultural policy. I was curious to record with them, to enter their laboratory, and above all I thought it would give me the chance to hear my own voice, to gain a record of it – even on my answering machine, I chose to defer to the voice server.

When I phoned the day before the recording session to ask them to send the text I would be reading so I might prepare a little, locate the unstable areas, the holes, the places I might speed up, one or the other of the Klangs put me firmly in my place: you'll see it when you read it, you'll let yourself be surprised – that's the only way to get in touch with this living matter that is language. Immediately, I found this wonderful – the words of a true artist. But the first verses and visual scan of the papers on the studio table unsettled me. "The Raven" by Edgar Allan Poe. I'd never read it. Eighteen verses. Baudelaire had translated it into French. This is what I was called here for? Inge (hat) started the recording: here we go, no effects, climb inside the text like you would through a half-open window, take your time to set up the darkness, the cracks in the floorboards, the dying fire, the solitude. I nodded, but then suddenly asked (the microphone amplifying my boldness): the narrator of the poem is a man, right? Sylvia (Rhodia notebook), surprised, let out a feral hiss: poetry has no gender.

I read two lines and Sylvia cut me off, curt, to ask me to read faster – avoid being solemn. Stream of silence. I counted three seconds in my head and started again. *Eagerly I wished the morrow; – vainly I had sought to borrow / From my books surcease of sorrow*, but I must have been going too fast, because in the second stanza I stumbled over my name, or rather a name so similar to my own I thought it was a spelling mistake: *sorrow for the lost Lenore*. Stunned, I turned towards the control room. Sylvia's voice, saccharine: it's a coincidence, Léonore, nothing more. Let's continue.

So I adjusted the distance between my mouth and the mic, which I saw as a friend, a hard friend, the kind that never lets anything happen to you, that gives you their full, singular attention, then I repositioned my headphones and started over, calm, feeling my breath shaping itself around the poem and seeing Inge's and Sylvia's faces expand as they listened on the other side of the glass, surprised. I read plainly and without drama, discovering the internal geometry of the text; I moved about inside it, and I still don't know what it was that broke my rhythm, why I tripped up right when I was saying: *Much I marveled this ungainly fowl to hear discourse so plainly, / Though its answer little meaning – little relevancy bore.* Inge pounded on her seat and Sylvia must have shouted: *Scheiße!* I didn't say anything – I remembered then that ravens could learn to speak, to imitate human voices, the howl of a wolf, the song of a blackbird, the engine of a car, and maybe even the cries of a child. Have a sip of water, Inge said. You're not drinking enough. Let's start over. From the top? I saw myself in the glass as though in a mirror, pale, circles carved deep under my eyes, forehead oily, and my red hair had taken on glints of tangerine. Sylvia was unyielding: start over from the first line, start the whole thing again.

I thought to myself: they want the whole text in one go, a vocal long take, pure, without edits, it's my voice they chose and they have all the time in the world. Suddenly I felt trapped in this cockpit, I wanted to get out of here, to leave these two madwomen and their raven of doom in the lurch. I started over, but the lines of the poem fell apart in my mouth. And the more I started over, the more I failed to read them, unable to get past the first stanzas, nervous, and the tension rose on the other side of the glass. Another mess-up, said Inge, let's take a break, and in the next moment, a little fridge at the back of the room spat out two flasks of vodka that the sisters unscrewed like bottles of syrup and knocked straight back.

I massaged my neck, and in an attempt to relax I thought about the process that converts breath into an articulated voice, and has done so for thousands of years: I pictured the larynx, low in my throat, and my vocal cords, these two pale little folds vibrating against each other at extraordinary speeds as air is breathed into the lungs; I imagined the alveoli, bronchi, trachea, and then the cavity, palate, teeth, and lips, and I broke down the transformation of these vibrations into a human voice, this voice the mic was now rendering with every slightest occlusion, the least fibrillation, the tiniest bit of fuzz; this voice that was at this moment saying: *Open here I flung the shutter, when, with many a flirt and flutter, / In there stepped a stately Raven of the saintly days of yore; / Not the least obeisance made he; not a minute stopped or stayed he; / But, with mien of lord or lady, perched above my chamber door – / Perched upon a bust of Pallas just above my chamber door – / Perched, and sat, and nothing more.* So I continued to read, but it wasn't my voice, it was someone else's, the voice of a stranger – I read the poem and felt the raven's feathers brushing against me now, touching my hair, caressing my forehead, and felt its claws on my shoulder like it was sitting on a perch, while the stanzas tumbled into the microphone one after another, *Nevermore! Nevermore!*

I read breathlessly, somnambulistic and perfectly oriented, as though I was racing ahead of the poem, and soon, as echolalia scrambled the language, I read as though I was afraid, an archaic fear, issued from the age of caves when the human ear was formed. At the end, silence hardened space, I fell back in the chair, exhausted, and used the tail of my shirt to wipe away tiny drops of sweat that had gathered along my temples, forehead, and the sides of my nose. A second later, Inge burst into the room trailing cigarette smoke and dry hair, and threw out her long arms like ropes towards the microphone: there's something off, there's a sound. I flinched, on the alert. A repeated scratch, a snag, audible only in the high frequencies, had ruined the take. Inge snatched the mic from its harness, strangled it in furious hands, took it apart, studied it, then proceeded to a series of tests with her sister, who remained on the control side, rigid before the screen where my voice was transformed into fluorescent bars. Can you read a line again? I read again: *This I sat engaged in guessing, but no syllable expressing / To the fowl whose fiery eyes now burned into my bosom's core.* Again. Again. Again. Start over. Behind the window,

Sylvia was shaking her head, it's the voice! she shouted, it's the voice that's messing up somehow.

I sat in a black leather armchair smoking, my legs folded under me. The control room, from this side of the glass, looked like the bridge of a spaceship – the consoles flashed and the lit screens showed kaleidoscopic forms that made my head spin. Smoking is very bad for the vocal cords, you know, said Inge, holding out her pack – Lucky Strikes. Everything was quiet now, we were drinking vodka in silence. Suddenly Sylvia got up to look at the sonogram again: the spectral trace of my voice undulated in waves as the recording played, a fluorescent orange line against the black and, like the nock of an arrow, a peak kept showing up at regular intervals, visible in the high notes. It's an old lesion – Sylvia Klang spoke with her face turned toward the computer, and you couldn't tell if she was addressing others or letting her inner voice be overheard, the one that thinks out loud. Then she said, her iris barely visible beneath lids pleated like old blinds: this dysphonia didn't exist on the first takes, it came back during the session. Inge blew a smoke ring toward the ceiling: it's an old vocal strain, an old hematoma, the trace of an accident. Did this story about a raven remind you of something? Sylvia stared at me in the dimness, then said, turning the computer off: it's a good take, we'll keep it. I picked up my coat, knotted my scarf around my neck, and as I started up the spiral staircase that would take me back to the surface of the world, one of the two sisters – Sylvia, I think – said behind me: it's midnight, it's cold out, get home quick.

Outside, it was winter. I walked back up the dead-end street toward Place Denfert, and everything around me seemed at once more caustic and more real. A few meters ahead, perched on a stone wall, a raven sat waiting. Powerful and utterly still. Feathers of bluish black, beak long and hooked, he looked at me with intense eyes glittering with curiosity. I moved forward, half dizzy, awestruck, probably a little drunk, and slid my fingers between the feathers: he was warm and full of life. Are you the Raven of the saintly days of yore? I whispered. He nodded his head, then let out a strange sound, a deep *raaak* that reverberated around us. I thought he looked friendly and smart, and as though to mark our first meeting, he opened his wings – a width of at least a meter – lifted off majestically, and the beaten night air mixed with December's cold.

# A Light Bird

TOWARD THE END of the meal, sentences began to tumble like stones onto the plates and, progressively, the thousands of infrasonic hissing sounds produced by two people eating together in the kitchen of an old apartment – scrape of cutlery against earthenware, creak of wicker chairs, glug-glug of water poured into glasses, bodily sounds – all this overtook the room. These changes in acoustic tone had come to signal that Lise was preparing to speak about her mother, and I instinctively pulled back. I saw her put down her cutlery, calmly wipe her mouth, lean forward, and turn her face toward me, cast in relief by the overhead light, and perhaps also

137

shaped by the face of Rose, whom she sometimes resembles in such a troubling (though fleeting) way. She caught my eye with such intensity it was no longer possible for me to evade her. Dad – I heard the agitation in her voice, controlled but audible, and the excess of solemnity that signals an imminent declaration: Dad, I want you to erase Mom's voice from the answering machine.

A current of icy air rushed past and I capsized against the back of the chair. For a few seconds I felt like a man standing on a frozen river that suddenly cracks and splits, fracture lines starring outward all around me, racing off as far as the eye could see. Lise's eyes did not leave mine as the silence rose between us, thicker and thicker, vehement. And then she placed her hand on mine, and repeated more slowly, please, do it now, put an end to this. She got up then to clear the table, turning her back to me, plunging her hands into the sink, making it clear that this dinner and this conversation were finished.

But I hadn't finished with her, nor with her mother's voice, this voice that can indeed be heard on the answering machine of the telephone in the apartment, even though my wife has been dead now for five years, one month, and twenty-seven days. So, leaning on the table, I stood in turn and shouted, no! – a distinct and round *no*, as dense and dull as a lead shot from a rifle at a fairground stand. Lise jumped, letting out a high, uncontrollable sound, and the cutlery she dropped bounced on the tiles in a clatter of metal. She gripped the edge of the sink, head down between her shoulders, neck outstretched, shoulder blades jutting beneath her pastel cotton top. She was breathing hard. I could see her reflected in the window that had become a mirror with the arrival of night, her eyes closed, mouth open, corners of her lips trembling with anger: my loving and reasonable daughter, my hard-edged girl.

This wasn't the first time she had asked me. And she wasn't the only one to ask, either. Others would often beat around the bush but finally admit they found it "unsettling" to hear Rose's voice on the answering machine – "unsettling," a twisted understatement; "indecent" or "morbid" would have been closer to what they meant, but they didn't have the courage to speak these words, felt they were sparing me, while I, of course, did not spare them. The pain of Rose's death, extended well beyond all propriety, pulverizing the limits set by social norms and the psychological slurry of magazines dedicated to well-being and mental health, this pain, but maybe also the desire I had to keep Rose in the hollow of my ear, irreducible, incarnate – this offended them now. The irruption of the voice of the dead into the world of the living undoes time, implodes borders, the natural order goes haywire, and the recorded voice of my wife played its part in this chaos. No matter how much I argued for my sovereignty over the old answering machine in my home, the intimacy of my relationship with her, with her death, with her voice, Lise always replied that my machine was a space open to all, a social intermediary. Don't you see it makes you look crazy? she murmured now, from the bottom of a well of sorrow, and when she finally turned toward me, her face was so close to mine that I could see myself reflected in her irises, bathed in tears.

*Hi, you've reached us, but we're not here; leave us a message and we'll call you back!* Like a light bird, Rose's voice moved through the room, brushing against walls, windows, shelves; it expanded into the space, conserving enough energy toward the end of the recording to produce a curious vibration, as though it were growing distant without being erased, diminishing without disappearing completely – the mysterious remanence of a fade-out.

Lise and I folded in on ourselves in the dark living room, like two blind people in a canoe, paddling countercurrent. Sitting on the ground, Lise waited for the message to end, head tipped back, eyes on the ceiling. Hers is the first voice I ever heard, she said, very calm, as though she were speaking these words from the depths of a dream. I knew it before I was even born, I could make it out among thousands of others. I clutched the armrest of the couch, taut, listening. Lise raised a hand to her temple and, eyes on the ground, intoned, it lives inside my ear, that voice, it has never left me, it's not erased and I'm not afraid of losing it: it's hers. At that moment, the lights of a car leaving the parking lot of the building across the street cast the room in a very yellow light – the ceiling seemed to grow round like a cupola, more vast, more sonorous, and in this shifting light I saw my child stand, suddenly brought back to grief, and all at once find the way in: her recorded voice is in the present moment forever, but it's a different present, a present in which her death hasn't happened, a present that will never coincide with mine, with my life, and it makes me crazy, it hurts, it hurts so much. After a silence, she spoke again, heart-rendingly: contrary to what you think, my grief gets stronger each time I have to hear the message, and it makes me stop calling you because I'm scared to hear it. Think of other people. Please, erase it.

*Hi, you've reached us, but we're not here – leave us a message and we'll call you back!* The night Rose died, when I got back from the hospital, I was sitting in this very same spot, already in darkness. When the first call came in and I heard those words – "you've reached us, but we're not here" – I started to shake, as though in all my life I had never heard a more naked truth: no, we weren't here, would never be again, it was over. The telephone rang until late into the night but I didn't answer, not once: I wanted to hear this voice return, this voice like none other, this voice that contained Rose completely, embodied though ethereal, physical as only a voice can be. But at dawn, having listened to it so many times, something else stirred in me: I imagined that Rose's voice had decamped at the very last moment from the body that sheltered it – that it had saved itself, so as not to become this cold corpse covered by a rough sheet – so it might return here (and so that this "us" might persist?) and continue, reactivated with each play, in a sort of infinite present. Her voice survived her, in recorded form, indestructible, in the form of a light bird. In the morning I realized there was no other recording of Rose's voice, and I kept it.

*Hi, you've reached us, but we're not here – leave us a message and we'll call you back!* From the very first word, the scene comes rushing back: the day before we left for Greece, the hurry to set up the answering machine, Rose in jeans and a striped T-shirt, feet bare, painted toenails, round sunglasses, and booklet open on her lap, following the instructions step by step to record the message, trying a few different formulations, laconic or overblown, and finally landing on this phrase, keeping the first take. It's a clear and golden voice, a voice from a Grecian Isle in

June, a voice dilated in a breath: the voice of a woman on the verge of leaving.

And yet, it's not this memory I'm trying to bring back when I phone the house, sometimes from the ends of the earth, sometimes in the middle of the night, just to connect for a moment to this sound, so real, to hear her inviting callers' messages, pronouncing that unforgettable "us" – this is what I answered Lise, who was waiting for me to speak and had come closer now, had rested her head against my knee, her fine blond hair creating a halo of brightness in the dark, her ear as delicate as a chickadee's nest. What I'm after, I told her, forcing myself to put simple words to the complex emotion that goes through me every time, what I'm after is the sense of her presence: Rose is here, quite simply. Of course I know the voice is not Rose, who is dead and won't come back, but for me, it's still a manifestation of her alive, the day she recorded this radiant message, the day before we left on vacation.

Is Rose's absence too present in my life? Does it take up too much space? Lise sometimes asks out loud whether the spectral envelope of my wife's voice hasn't become a morbid passion. She says I'm in the grip of her ghost, suggests a denial of reality, even claimed the other day that I was trying to keep the dead alive – and I liked that expression, I recognized it as true. And yet it's Lise who's still wearing her mother's slip-on shoes, the putty-colored trench coat that makes her look like a passenger of the night, the oversized men's shirts, and even her gloves – she's the one ferreting about in the traces her mother leaves behind. For some time now, she's been talking about Rose's last trip – Rose would go away for a few weeks each year, alone, with her drawing book, pencils, and camera – talking about taking the same trains, making stopovers in the same places, pausing to contemplate the same landscapes. Even though it pains me, I encourage her: these concrete actions that continue to form links between the living and the dead, beyond cemeteries, beyond urns forgotten in the shadows of alcoves, beyond anniversaries and frames that hold photographs of the dead on the walls of houses, in plain view of everyone, these actions that call us to rise, secretly, to the height of absence, always seem to me more unfettered, and above all more analgesic than the painful abstraction of grief.

Lise cried silently for a long time, and I cried with her – my only child. This had never happened, one of us had always kept our eyes dry, probably so as to better help the other. And I knew then that I could do it: put time back in order. That the moment had come to relieve my daughter, by becoming the man who couldn't be called crazy any longer. Everything happened very quickly: I got up and walked to the machine, arm outstretched, about to press the red button, ready to erase the tape with just one finger – but at that moment, caught off guard, Lise shouted: wait! Her voice pulled me back just in time, and I saw her dark shape move through the shadows in a rush: she grabbed my cell phone from the desk, punched in the passcode – Rose's birth date – opened the voice recorder, pushed play on the answering machine, and Rose's voice took wing again in the room, flew along the corniches, down near the ground, past the windows; it soared for a long moment, and Lise recorded it, as it migrated from the answering machine into my phone's memory, became an archive. And then she did exactly the same thing with her phone – it's for me, she murmured, concentrating, her irises very black beneath bronze eyelids.

An instant later, the recording of Rose's recorded voice – this double capture – became in my ear something else entirely: a woman on the verge of leaving announced our absence, sounding her faraway vibration from this night-time room where we had spoken, side by side, Lise and I, and cried together. You can erase it now – our daughter looked at me in the darkness, intent, the phone resting against her solar plexus. I pressed the red button and freed the light bird.

# After

THIS BEER CAP rolling around in my mouth, little crown of corrugated metal, dented by a bite, its contour serrated with points, the top polished and the enamel smooth against my tongue, the underside rough, and the way the taste lingers – warm pocket change, hay and hops – the way it reminds you of bitterness; this Heineken gold piece stamped with a red-star tumbles against my teeth and I press it to my palate like a covert host. It's noon, the prairie crackles, a great silence reigns, the sky is strewn with photometeors, I'm dragging a large black plastic garbage bag, and before me, the flattened trampled grass marks out a lighter stretch in the vegetation, a vast basin where the stones that encircled our firepit last night are still warm.

It's a mess. Torn open chip bags, beer bottles, cans, and juice boxes, pizza boxes smeared with grease and melted cheese, slices of melon, cherry pits, masses of cigarette butts, marshmallows fallen in the dirt, a pink rubberband, a balled-up T-shirt that stinks of vomit, empty tobacco packets, charred stones, and this huge pile of flaky greyish ashes studded with bits of charcoal. Last night there were fifteen of us here rolling in the grass, dancing around the fire, drinking and smoking; some played astronomer and named the stars, tracing constellations with an index finger, others made out quietly in the shadows, and some sang shamelessly – but above all, we shouted. Shouts that didn't sound anything like the ones you let loose at summer concerts in the fairground, or like the ones hollered out in stadium stands on game days or in buses coming back on winning nights – shouts that weren't trying to stand together, to raise up a compact mountain range that would fill space and affirm its power; and these shouts had nothing to do, either, with cries of joy – of this I'm certain: we were relieved, hammered, devoured by terror, but we were not joyful.

So yes, yesterday: the final exam results. Lists posted in the school courtyard by late morning, the first shouts ringing out – high, excited, impatient squeals – those of us who rushed forward and those who stayed back, ostensibly taking their time to finish a cigarette (could they really care so little about what came next: repeat a year in this big country high school, or move on elsewhere, could they really just go on puffing like that, relaxed?) and me in the midst of all this, caught up in the movement of the crowd and then crushed against the results sheets, winded, nose pressed to the paper, finger sliding down each line, eyes ricocheting from name to name, and suddenly that strange howling that drilled through my throat, the clamor growing louder around me, names being called out, repeated louder into cell phones, the parents – the mothers – waiting off to the side in the parking lot behind the wheel, the relief, the tears and, spread from mouth to mouth, the conjugation of the verb "to get" in the present indicative – I got it, you got it, she got it, we got it – because in the end, everyone in the group got it, aside from Max, who dropped out in April, and Vinz, for whom all this is total bullshit.

I ran through the school gates and jumped on my bike without looking back, five kilometers down this road more familiar than even my mother's voice, and which was suddenly evasive, distant, like a laminated picture under a transparent film – the old roads of silent stones stretching out from too-black pavement, the garden-level pavilions, the façades in pale pink or salmon, the narrow rooftops, the piles of cinderblocks, here and there an inflatable pool for kids, a couple of dogs behind the fence, a trio of scrawny trees, but always a garage through which you enter the house; next, the crops appear, corn and sunflowers, and the further you get from the village, the more the countryside sows ruins: abandoned garages, tobacco hangars padded with ivy, tractors rusted to the color of Coca-Cola, cisterns devoured by ruderal flora, deserted farmhouses, poor and sagging houses, real hovels. I was thinking this was the last time I would make this trip, that I would never do it again, but instead of exulting, mouth open, taking off like a rocket, bye-bye countryside, something began to form in the pit of my larynx, a hitch, a scratch – I thought I had swallowed a bug and even stopped on the side of the road to spit. No one was home at my house. I took a long drink from the tap, leaning over halfway into the sink, then tipped my head back and stared at the ceiling as I gargled. I wanted to find my own clear voice again, the voice of a graduate getting ready to leave home, but instead of heading out onto the terrace and waiting in the sun with a smoke, cigarette held up behind my ear, star of the day, I went up to my room, closed the curtains and lay down shivering

in fetal position on my bed, eyes open, and in the bluish half-light, my room, too, looked strange to me, the
walls withdrawn, far off – it was the room of the girl I no
longer was, the girl I had ceased to be, and this was how
my mother found me when she got back at lunchtime –
curled up in a ball. What's wrong, are you coming down?
I sat up and answered that I had felt tired all of a sudden,
stress, the pressure of waiting for the results – I was lying:
I had been sure I would pass – and I went downstairs.

They were there, all three of them, standing in the
kitchen with the bottle of champagne open on the
counter – my father, my mother, and my brother Abel
who suddenly felt the urge to say something, make a
toast to me, mark the occasion, so we all stiffened and fell
silent, eyes on him, attentive – my mother surprised but
beaming because he was taking the initiative, embarking
on a solemn proclamation; he got into position, lifted
his glass to the height of his cheek, and that's when I
noticed that he'd changed, had put on a clean shirt, thir-

teen going on fifteen, lanky, lunar, and this way he had of smiling with the corner of his mouth, how pleased he was to surprise us, and I felt the pain in my throat come back, the flood of emotion, but then he grew overwhelmed, too – knowing that from now on it was over, I was going to leave – and he choked up on the first syllable, lips drawn back around a sound that repeated, again and again, insisting, but couldn't manage to draw out the next sounds behind it, towing the word along, the sentence, the proclamation he had risked, and the flow of his words was annihilated with the first breath as though the dozens of sessions with the speech therapist, the muscle development of the vocal tract, the breathing exercises, as though all method had evaporated, language had fled my brother's mouth, and this absence resonated in the room; my father stood with his arms crossed, pressing his glass to his chest, eyes on the floor tiles, lips closed, probably fighting to not finish the toast himself – the toast that was now becoming an ordeal, because at this point Abel was treading water, couldn't even begin his declaration, and the meaning of his words, his loving intention, all this was running towards me, speeding, while he himself remained far behind, and the more he tried to catch up, to be in synch, the more I heard the chaos that was drowning his palate, phonemes catapulted against teeth, ricocheting off each other and now form- ing something like an impenetrable cork – g, g, good, g, good – his sentence was emerging so slowly it was making me crazy, and sometimes he even went backwards, going back to ram that goddamn first syllable again that was blocking the way, and I stared at him with all my might to encourage him on, nodding my head emphatically, sharp little blows in the atmosphere at each of his attempts, because it seemed like he was butting into a wall to try and find the way out, an opening, his face twisted in a grimace now, distorted, cheekbones tense and trembling with each attempt, temples damp, and his black gaze so intense he could have disintegrated the old birdcage in his line of sight – good, good, good luck to my b, b, b, to my b, b, to my big s, s, s, sister – I couldn't stand it anymore, I wanted to unstop that mouth, put my brother out of his misery, so I opened my own and moved my lips to mime the articulation of the word that wouldn't come – I didn't let out a sound, but still my mother, just by her very presence and the explosive tension in her body, ordered me to stop that right away, to shut it and wait, because Abel wasn't giving up. The champagne splashed from his flute with each effort but still he persisted, and when he had finally spoken his whole sentence, reeling, shirt and fingers splattered with champagne, triumphing over language like a storm – farewell to my big sis who passed, she's off to college at last – we drank as though nothing had happened.

It was still light out when they pulled up in the yard, one full car and a few scooters driven bareheaded, Naples-style, extra passengers riding sidesaddle on the luggage racks. Everyone was there, the light was green, strangely dark, like the light inside a tropical greenhouse, I was wearing a pink cotton dress with thin straps and a pair of sneakers, and the air was heavy. A few minutes later we were walking behind the car that drove slowly along the road and then we entered the meadow – more than three hectares in one piece – with our load of logs and bottles, sleeping bags and blankets, chips and cookies, chicken sandwiches, hard liquor and an envelope of something to smoke, and then our gang stepped into the circle my father had mowed for us and set to work building the fire, a few guys offered to get it going, fought with each other, wasted matches, one of them asked me for some paraffin cubes, and in the end it was me who dug the pit, set up short dry logs in a cross, added pieces of crates and kindling, and lit the fire with Vinz's lighter.

Against my mother's advice (she had asked him to leave us alone), my father came by around eleven o'clock to see if everything was okay. Hey there, graduates. He shook everyone's hand, congratulated each one, joked with Max who put on a good face while I murmured through gritted teeth, okay Dad, that's enough, leave us alone, it's our graduation night, but he pretended not to hear, comparing the exams to a rite of passage, and then bummed a cigarette from Vinz – here, pass me a smoke, would ya – he took a couple drags, then flicked the filter into the fire, and just before he disappeared into the night, he tossed out this curious incitement to the company at large: make as much noise as you want. And then the music built up, we all pressed in together, seizing this last opportunity, this final chance, because at dawn we would disperse, everyone would be off into their life. In the orangey glow of the flames, our skin took on the gleam of fruit, some of us dripping, some singing in chorus, some rolling a quick joint, and only a few of us cried, mouth of the can jostling against our lips. And then Vinz, who was twenty, the oldest of the gang (which is what gave him his prestige), stood up in his red T-shirt and jeans lacerated across the thighs, and proposed, as a game, that everyone let out a scream. What the hell? Noëlla frowned. For once we're allowed to holler, gotta take advantage, he said, laughing. I thought of Abel, who'd had so much trouble uttering his declaration, and stopped listening to Vinz who was now telling the others how screaming had been banished from society, eliminated from our lives, confined to a few particular spaces – when you scream, you tip over onto the animal side, that's the problem, he concluded, making his eyes big and round and letting out the *ooh ooh*s of a primate.

The strange ritual began when the fire had thinned to an incandescent vertical spiral of great beauty: one by one, we each stepped into the darkness, then reappeared walking quickly towards the flames and stopped in front of the others to let out our scream – of terror, excitement, despair, anger, or pleasure: pleas, barks, and vociferations. You should try the primal scream too, Vinz whispered in my ear as he flicked his cigarette into the fire. I looked at him, startled, whatever, but he got caught up in it: pretend you're being born – let out a powerful cry, and that's it, you're reborn, no more sadness, sweet deal! Oh yeah, sure. When it was my turn, I stepped out into the shadows, and I went far, walking through the tall grasses, feeling the paths made by the deer, the trenches where the wild boar had urinated, copulated, where the sows had given birth, I walked diagonally towards the cistern, and the air was insanely dense, bugs stuck to my damp skin by the dozen, mosquitoes sucked my blood, I felt the pulse of the meadow, its wild vibration, and I listened for a long time, apart from humans, close to the animals, and then came back to the party which, from far off, resembled a flare, and screamed in my turn – I shouted, I yelled until my voice broke, and then I fell asleep.

It sounded like monkeys, that's what my mother said this morning as she flipped through an old issue of *National Geographic* with her long thoughtful hand, we could hear you from here and you know what? You would have thought it was chimpanzees. I had just come down to the kitchen – when I woke up that morning I discovered I was mute, my vocal cords not stirring anymore, and so I was unable to contradict her other than by a wheeze, a skeptical pout, a shrug. I sat down across from her and while she wandered again through the dog-eared pages marked with blue ballpoint pen, I observed her long, angular, expressive face, her dark hair hastily twisted atop her head with a pen or a chopstick, her large cambered eyelids and blond, feathery lashes. Before going out I lifted the cover of her magazine, certain that I would find, inside the golden-yellow frame of this American monthly she must have pored over hundreds of times, the photo of a young blond woman in her thirties, sitting in the foliage among primates – Jane Goodall, 1965. The woman who speaks to chimpanzees. Then my mother got up, imperial in her purple robe, and handed me the garbage bag.

I reach between the warm grasses that trap the detritus, fingers shaping the primitive grip (a suspicious grip, vaguely disgusted), the meadow hums, a bitter scent emanates from the ground, heady, humidity of baked mulch. I collect the burned-down matches and hairpins, an earring, a pillowcase, a flyer for canoe rentals at the river, a broken knife and a pack of contraceptive pills, a banana peel, a phone case, chicken carcasses – smooth, whitish bones, so perfectly cleaned you would have thought they'd been regurgitated from the mouth of a fox. A dry snap off in the brushwood – I lift my head: a sparrowhawk shoots from the woods and rises into the sky in ascending flight, and I instinctively turn towards the cistern, to the north: there's Abel, in the lichen, this is where he always goes to sing, and maybe he's watching me now, too, as I pace across the plot with this black bag swinging in the hot air, this bag I fill with remnants, remains, these small things.

# Ontario

IT's a November evening in Toronto. I'm eating alone on the thirty-eighth floor of a hotel beside Lake Ontario – pale-green linguine alle vongole, rolled up in a ball in the hollow of a deep plate with disproportionate edges.

I arrived late, there's almost no one left here, and the room is quiet as though someone had just cut the music. I've been seated at a table placed slightly apart beside the long bay window, a table with a nice view, the hostess said, banana chignon and patent-leather pumps, before returning to her podium over by the door. One of the servers quickly whisked away the other place setting from my table as though it were written on my forehead that I wasn't expecting anyone, and this plate, indecent, emphasizing my aloneness, was wrecking the ambience: and how are you today? Liquid voice, standard pleasantries, he can't be more than twenty, acne on his temples, hair gelled into little vertical points that sparkle under the overhead lights. I ordered wine, wanted to pronounce the words "cabernet sauvignon" in my terrible English, wanted to signal that I was a foreigner, wanted to be a woman in the night sitting in the sky somewhere in a North American megapolis, far from her family, far from home.

Outside, electricity rewrites space. The diurnal city, ordinary, vertical, is transformed: thousands of lights perforate the skyscrapers, but Lake Ontario, as I see it at this moment, could be located elsewhere, far, somewhere kilometers away from this city whose edges it laps at without reflecting the lights, nothing, not a single spark, not a flash, barely an iridescent edge or a vague gleam at the base of the towers along Lake Shore Boulevard and beside the wharves.

The young server sets down a tulip glass before me that could have held an entire bottle, in which my wine forms a thin, red, reflective deposit – a miniature lake – at the bottom, and just then two men arrive at the entrance and are soon led to a table near mine, a table with a nice view, repeats the hostess on autopilot, probably worn out, in a hurry to get home, her feet killing her, and they sit down heavily and loosen their ties. They are tall and massive, tired suits under long trench coats, thick necks, bellies hanging over their belts, signet rings on their middle fingers and poppies in their buttonholes. I immediately recognize the one facing me in three-quarter profile, his horse-like head, prominent eyeballs and convex teeth, dark yellow like old ivory: he frowns at the menu, then leans back in his chair and scans the room with his eyes, stopping on mine for a fraction of a second, trying to remember where we might have met.

Just this afternoon, there was a crowd in the Brigantine Room at the Harbourfront Centre where we were celebrating the opening of the festival, glasses in hand and lanyards around our necks labeling the bodies. Faye, a translator from Winnipeg who specializes in Indigenous literatures, had sent a text asking me to meet her there and, swallowed up in this gathering where I didn't know anyone, I clung madly to our rendezvous as the thing that justified my presence. The tangle of voices formed a floating mattress the size of the hall, a thick, fibrous layer, punctured here and there by the exclamations that go along with reunions, names called out, laughter high and sharp like the head of a pin, a vaguely animal murmur that I walked through lengthwise, immersed, and emerged at the other end of the hall behind the buffet where I leaned against a wall, slightly apart, and kept watch for Faye – I had met her before the summer at a translation workshop and had accompanied her through the streets of Arles in search of a banjo so she could play "Over the Waterfall" at the wrap party.

I watched what happened from behind the white table-cloths, the pacing of the servers, the merry-go-round of sneakers worn with work trousers, the boxes of bottles torn open one after another, the bags of chips and crackers ripped open and poured continuously into metal salad bowls, large garbage bags where paper napkins and translucent plastic cups were tossed, when all at once a subtle change in the acoustics signaled that something was happening over at the back of the hall behind the compact barrier formed by the people standing at the buffet, as though a sound wave had swept the space, and I saw a few heads turn as though from the jolt of an electrical stimulus, saw eyebrows raise and noses lift above heads, and I thought maybe someone had fainted in the back, a fall, or maybe a spat between two people, an insult, an alcohol-fueled scuffle, but it was something else, it was silence that drilled its hole through the crowd, smashing through the clamor, slowly driving bodies toward the walls of the hall, progressively enlarging a circle big enough for a high-pitched voice to be heard, a voice with such a sharp and sensitive texture it made me think of a Shibata diamond oscillating at the bottom of the microgroove on a vinyl record, the mineral needle always finer, stronger, seeking out pure contact at the bottom of a dark fold, total contact.

*We are the Dead. Short days ago / We lived, felt dawn, saw sunset glow, / Loved and were loved, and now we lie, / In Flanders fields.* For a few moments the pointed voice etched itself on the silence, undulating and solitary, reactivating rings of memory one by one, and then a few mouths began to move, abdomens swelled beneath shirts, necklaces slid over throats, ice cubes clinked, and soon other voices joined the first, coming to wind around it as though caught in its centrifugal force, and together they recited the end of the poem in unison. From where I stood, I saw the expressions on the faces change as something moved over them, something from the past that returned now, but I understood nothing of this collective declamation taking place in the middle of a hall where, just a few minutes earlier, everyone seemed busy making plans for the week in an rippling buzz, peering at electronic calendars – BlackBerries, iPhones – screens displaying not literary panels or events, but lunches and drinks, dates that would happen in the interstices of the festival, in its discreet margins, where one might negotiate an advance on a book to be translated, an assignment of movie rights, or even transfers of authors, editors, and agents. When the voice stopped, there was a sort of collective holding of breath, total silence, and then the crowd broke out in applause and I caught a glimpse of the woman standing there in the middle of the space created, a tall gangly silhouette in a red wool dress and leather boots, shoulders hunched, head down, quivering, out of breath, clutching a whiskey glass between two hands as the crowd closed around her, causing her to disappear – I hadn't recognized Faye's voice.

A little while later, I decided to go over to the buffet and try to nab an hors d'oeuvre, a mouthful, a piece of cake, anything that might occupy my hands and mouth as I waited for her to reappear. There you are! I spun around and Faye was smiling at me, gracious, lifting her glass up to eye level in a silent toast which I returned: all that was missing was the banjo to accompany you – what was that poem, anyway? She grinned with her eyes wide like a kid who's just done something silly, and translated the first lines aloud, arm held out over the buffet for another ginger ale. It was a popular poem, a poem that everyone here knew, composed by a Canadian military doctor for the funeral of his friend who died in the Second Battle of Ypres, May 1915: Flanders fields, fields of honor, fields devastated by shells, fields where bodies of

men and animals lay rotting, fields of blood, fields of poppies. Faye drank and spoke quickly, but I recognized her
distinctive phrasing, her particular way of accelerating at
the end of the sentence, compressing the syllables and
sending them forth with fervor, the way someone might
throw shovelfuls of earth over their shoulder.

The Brigantine Room began to clear out, everyone
looking at their watches, knotting their scarves, signal-
ing an imminent departure, while the servers cleared the
buffet, scrunching up dirty napkins. But Faye lingered.
She poured herself another glass, grabbing the bottle by
the neck, and as she scanned the hall for someone who
hadn't turned up, she spoke to me of poppies, which
only grow in limestone soil, on ground that's been disturbed, turned over, aerated – often they'll spring up on
battlefields ravaged by combat, flourish on mass graves
or around tombs, did you know that? She didn't like the
war poem all that much, the way the memory of the dead
was linked (as so often) to the exhortation to continue

175

fighting – propaganda! she smiled, rolling the *r*, fiddling with a pack of Chesterfields which she finally opened with her teeth – but she pointed to the felt poppy on the collar of her dress, look, everyone's wearing one today, it's Remembrance Day. And then she froze: the man with the horse's head was there, just a few meters away, and was staring at her, standing stock still in his big black coat. Their eyes met, they seemed to be silently making a date to meet later on, and then he turned to go and Faye followed him with her eyes, murmuring, nose in her glass, there you have it, it's the day of the dead here, it's Poppy Day.

The restaurant lights dim, and my table is plunged into shadow as though the ceiling bulbs had all spontaneously bust. On my plate, in a play of contrast between materials, the linguine becomes green kelp, almost phosphorescent, tangled. A ball of lake grass with tiny shells that also reminds me, now that I think of it, of the lines in a brain, the way they're drawn in sagittal slices in old natural science manuals, their sinuous mnemic circuits like electric wires, these other rings of memory. I untangle them slowly, trace their path, work them with my fork.

A few meters away, the man with the horse's head is sharing a chinook salmon with his companion. The young server motions with his head toward the bay window: it was caught out there, in this very lake. Then, suddenly excited, voluble, he launches into a presentation on the annual stocking of Lake Ontario, fish farming and the salmon migration, extraordinary fish, truly, fish that can travel more than three thousand kilometers to return to the spawning grounds, from the Yukon estuary, for example, all the way to upstream of Whitehorse – my father, who loved to fish and was familiar with the marvelous complexity of the water system around the Great Lakes, would undoubtedly have asked this young man to sit down and tell him more, would have compared material and told him about his catches, and in a rush of panic

I called my father's voice back to my ear, his high-pitched and mineral voice that was heard so rarely at the end, I fought for it to come back now because strangely, far more than a photograph or any other object that might make me see their beloved faces, it was by remembering the voices of the dead that I could keep them present in me – the young server's gestures grow more and more dramatic, he forgets himself, until the man with the horse's head interrupts him in a flat voice: amazing.

When we left the center after the cocktail party on opening night, Faye insisted we go out in a boat on the lake – it's wonderful, you'll see. I hedged, hadn't adjusted to the time zone, was afraid I'd be cold, but she took me by the wrist and chirped that I couldn't leave Toronto without going out on the sparkling lake – in Kanien'kéha, one of the Iroquoian languages that Faye translates, *ontario* means something like "lake of shining waters." She led me to Bathurst Quay, to the marina under the yacht club where her cousin, who had just opened a small sport-fishing business, was waiting for us aboard a Chris-Craft Commander. Once we were on board, Julius – a peaceful giant with a ZZ Top beard and hoodie with a cannabis leaf on the chest – tossed each of us a smelly, freezing-cold life vest and we set sail, and then Toronto rose up on the shore, the CN Tower, the Rogers Center dome, the Harbourfront skyscrapers. Faye gave me a radiant look – not bad, eh?

The lake was frankly not shining, the water was rather murky and, veiled in grey, the city watched us from on high like a futurist movie set, hostile and powerful. At one point Faye pointed out past the front of the boat, exclaiming: if we kept going that way, we'd reach Niagara Falls! I immediately pictured the washtub from the movies that had terrified me as a child, the western where a young boy is closed up in a barrel and tossed into the rapids. I thought of the hypnotic force of the falls, the attraction they have for some people who end up throwing themselves in, and of everything that disappears, pulverized in the great churning of the end. I shouted to Faye that now was the time to launch into "Over the Waterfall," but the volume of the motor and the crash of the bow on the lake were so loud it was impossible to hear each other, so I mimed the banjo player, fingers racing over the invisible instrument and the fast nasal voice bouncing along like a ball on a sheet metal roof, and she laughed, her little otter eyes creasing. I took shelter in a corner in the back, but she, oddly, went up to the front, right in the wind, face exposed to the spray, eyes closed, utterly absorbed in the elements, and then frothy points covered the surface of the water, the sky darkened, and the shore was hidden in the mist. The boat listed, I was tossed about, disoriented, but somehow I ended up dozing there, head nodding against the cabin wall.

When I opened my eyes again, Faye was leaning over the rail, half her torso over, and she seemed to be looking for something at the bottom of the lake – I wondered what she was up to and looked over at Julius through the bridge window, but his expression gave nothing away, he stood straight, headphones on, one hand on the wheel, a bottle of Coors at his lips, very calm. I joined him in the cabin where the smell of beer and fish mixed with that of fuel, he checked his position on the GPS and murmured, that's it, we're in the zone, then slowed his speed until he cut the motor, at which point I saw Faye take her red paper poppy from her coat and throw it into the lake where it floated for a time before disappearing, swallowed up by the black water. I held my breath, bewildered, and in spite of the sounds from outside that swelled in the cabin, I heard Julius whisper something like "poor Faye," adding, "her little girl, it's just awful," his face crumpling, and I thought he might burst into tears. A sudden roll startled us, stronger than the others, and I stumbled. Get inside now! Julius shouted, sticking his head out the door, and when Faye didn't react, he honked the horn and I saw her turn and come toward us, smiling, her eyes red and wet locks of hair stuck to her temples. Thanks, Julius. A hard little rain drummed on the surface of the lake, striated like an old zinc plate. The three of us crowded into the cabin, Julius wasn't sure he had enough fuel to get all the way to Niagara-on-the-Lake and so we turned around, the trip was over. In the saloon, I saw cans of beer and salt-and-vinegar chips, the open pack of Chesterfields, kitchen twine, boxes of hooks, oilskins rolled up in balls, and then I went up closer to see the few newspaper clippings taped to the wall: Julius posing after a fishing trip holding salmon as big as Cadillacs.

The shore reappeared as night was falling, a dark forest that reminded me of the roughness of sandpaper, sloping gently towards the lake. From time to time, a boat tied to a wooden dock signaled an isolated house, the windows dark. I came out of the cabin where Faye was phoning her mother, as she did every Saturday, while Julius smoked his evening joint. I needed some air. The wind had died down and we were moving slowly, the water so flat that the boat's path formed a steady gather, like a piece of fabric draped over a body. Far off we could see Toronto by night, lit up, but around me the world remained opaque, enigmatic, traversed by invisible presences. The call of a coyote from the depths of the woods pierced the silence. I thought of a contact call, the call of an individual that's isolated, separated from its family, waiting for a response. When we were back at the quay, Faye placed her hands on my shoulders and said, her voice once again very high and very direct – the voice she'd used this very afternoon in the Harbourfront Centre when she recited the poem: you'll remember Ontario, won't you?

I didn't think I would see her again before I left. But before going up to eat on the thirty-eighth floor, I went back to the pub on the pier to pick up an adapter I had left, and there she was. The room was full, and the waxed mahogany tables with large golden hinges like shackles on a boat evoked the warm ambience of port bars. I went up to the counter, and there in front of the fireplace, their profiles glowing orange before the flames, I saw her and the man with the horse's head, face to face above golden-brown whiskies that seemed enormous to me. Their legs were entwined below the table, but their chests and eyes kept their distance. On this table as on the others, a basket was full of paper poppies that Faye picked up absently one after the other and flicked across the table, until suddenly the man with the horse's head got up and threw them all into the fire. Then they both lowered their heads, stricken.

I'm the only one left in here, the restaurant is empty, the lights are out. I hear voices in the kitchens. The man with the horse's head left with his friend, their drinks unfinished and napkins fallen onto the carpet. But I'm not finished yet, I'm lingering, certain, now, that the glass walkway at the top of a Toronto skyscraper is the site of a secret rendezvous.

I don't like lakes. It's probably the thought of stagnant

water, moldering. Of drowned gulfs, Gates to Hell lurking in the abyss, the Loch Ness Monster – the creature forgotten at the bottom of prehistoric waters who wakes up hungry. The summer I turned seven, one of my aunts shouted over lunch that polio was in the neighboring lake, one of the kids from the area had caught it, and all the evenings that followed, double locked into a spartan bathroom, I scrutinized my skin and waited for the apparition of an unknown illness in my body; much later, during a personality test for a position as a salesgirl in a large store, I calmly associated the word "lake" with the word "death," but it wasn't the response they were looking for and my interviewer had a slight recoil, you have some dark ideas! If I had said "clarity" I might have had more luck, or maybe "canoe."

When I think back on it, it's strange that I didn't associate lake and canoe: at home, in my apartment, there's a canoe hanging in the entry hall. It was made in the traditional way, quick, light, birch-bark hull, interior and gunwales lined with cedar strips, caulked with pine resin gum and grease, and built, indeed, on the shores of Lake Ontario – as the certificate of authenticity pinned to the inside will attest. The day it was delivered by UPS truck, ten years ago, everyone in the apartment gathered around the package, aghast at what seemed such a cumbersome thing, an object whose delivery by plane had cost a fortune and which, unwrapped in the middle of the living room, looked exactly like a whim – mine – and then we found it a place at the intersection of the hallways where it still hovers, without nail or rope, its supple material making it possible to wedge it between two walls, holding and resisting them – holding and resisting them, that's just what I said to myself. Is this ours? said the little boy with dark-chocolate eyes who watched the scene, astounded to see us installing a canoe on the ceiling.

I pick up my bag, my phone, and my scarf, and stand to press my forehead to the bay window. The lake is no more than a dark flatness, a kind of screen on which I can make out the back of my father's fishing cabin, his bamboo rods, reels, nets, and silver hooks, and, tacked to the wall, this image I've known forever: a man alone on calm water, standing tall, fishing, the wake of his canoe tracing its microgroove on the shining water; a sepia photograph on which my father had written in blue ballpoint pen: "Iroquois man on Lake Ontario."

# Arianespace

I T'S THE LAST one in the village. Rumor has it she's outlived everyone and chased away the rest, that's how they talk about her in these parts, where her first name is all that's needed: Ariane. According to the police report, she is ninety-two years old, and what I hope, as I park my car at the end of the path, is that her memory will still be accessible and that she'll have the desire to tell – but those who talk too easily, and pull out stories like rabbits from a hat, are not always the most credible witnesses, as we all know from experience.

I like arriving at people's houses on foot, like a neighbor, or someone familiar enough to show up unexpectedly, just passing by. Before knocking, I look around a little, take the measure of the place, note the perspectives, the blind spots and vanishing lines, locate the landmarks. The only road in the village, with its central grassy crest between two black mud furrows, slopes gently upward between abandoned buildings, chaos of fallen-in roofs and walls, cluttered in sections by heavy rubble and solitary stones. I tried as I walked to take note here and there of a door, a window, an intact façade so as to reconstitute their layout, their size, and imagine them approximately. These ruins, which had once been human habitations, were now thick with lichen and moss, overrun by bindweed and nettles, and emitted a low continuous vibration which I confused with silence. Surprised, I imagined the mice and garter snakes that scurried or darted behind me, while the ants and worms returned to their manufacturing deep within underground galleries. The air was

acidic, the weather heavy, the sky white; something powdery floated in the atmosphere. Ariane's house, which I
had located on a satellite map, towered over this rubble.

At the sound of the buzzer, I entered a small cement
courtyard lined with seedlings in pots, a white plastic
chair, and a broom. I waited, bending my knees to peer
through the window in the door. Ariane came up behind
me, a fluorescent pink basin in her arms, her voice low
and clear: are you looking for me? I let out a little shriek
and whipped around like a kid caught in the act. With
a disproportionate hand covered in brown spots, she
pushed away my investigator's card from TFSNAP (Task
Force for the Study of Non-identified Aerospace Phe-
nomena), and I followed her into the kitchen – coded
mayhem, remains of human life – and the next minute we
were sitting down to a café au lait, served in large grooved
bowls. I took out a notebook, the form, and a pen, and
then, once Ariane's civil status was established, I asked

her to tell me what she'd seen the night of the twenty-first to the twenty-second of June. I was surprised to see her get up to fetch a pack of smokes and become a completely different person with a cigarette in her mouth.

I had imagined her small and wizened, the wrinkled skin of an old fig, hair sparse, body brittle and slow, an apron tied around her waist and black peasant stockings, but she was something else: a tall, regal woman in jeans, a red T-shirt, and boots, and she was thin, long grey hair over her shoulder, cheekbones still high, and beneath ragged eyelids, eyes of a deep black – the kind of black that absorbs nearly all visible light, and which is found in bird of paradise feathers or on the belly of peacock spiders; altogether wizened, dry, and flaking, but conveying a great impression of physical strength and brutality.

I asked her to describe her sighting, just that: what did it look like? She finished her cigarette in silence. I couldn't take my eyes off the hard veins taut as electric cables under her skin. I thought she was trying to find a way to begin, and to help her, I blurted out the criteria for good camouflage which I'd learned in the army: shape, shadow, movement, brightness, colors? Her eyes moved to meet mine, and I blinked to escape them. She blew smoke toward the ceiling: I know what I saw.

That night, the night of the summer solstice, when she'd opened the window in her room to draw closed the outside shutters, a luminous shape was gliding slowly over the abandoned rooftops, red underneath – like the ring on the gas cooker, she said, gesturing to the stove with her chin – with a bunch of green spots on top. It was flying low, without a sound. The stars weren't out yet and its shape was clearly outlined, a flattened cone shape, or that of a turtle, the shape of a flying saucer. I asked to see the window. She went ahead of me into a plain room, wooden floors and whitewashed walls, and I noticed above her narrow bed a model of the ocean liner SS *France* placed on a shelf beside a Grundig transistor radio. Seen from above, the village was thick with brambles, folded in on itself beneath time, and the view did indeed include a large stretch of sky. Ariane added, calm, it was very beautiful, you know, those red and green lights. It made me think of the lights of New York. From what I had learned about her, Ariane had spent her whole life within a thirty-kilometer radius of this place.

The complexity of human testimony strikes me even more, now, than the observed facts themselves. Now, my penchant for the faraway absolute has been erased in favor of a leaning toward the nearby, and I envision these stories of sightings, these prosaic and fragile little narratives collected for over twenty years from all across the country, as the true substance of cosmic wonder. The emotions that are wrapped up in them – from a rush of excitement or panicked fear to unbridled megalomania – the entanglement of dreams and lived memories, the blending of time frames, the summary interpretation charts, the hasty deductions, the optical and autokinetic illusions, the cases of retinal persistence, the errors of estimation of distance, the choice of vocabulary, the beliefs, the metaphysical fiber of the witness, all of this captivates me as much as the UFOs themselves. But I joined TFSNAP because of my passion for ufology, and probably also because in March 1986 I had missed the passage of Halley's comet – I was fifteen, I kept watch every night from the window of my room, not realizing it was parading through the southern hemisphere, in fact; I would imagine it coming into my room at the speed of light and dragging along the entire cosmos in its wake, black holes, galaxies, planets, and possible lives, and then I would integrate the very movement of the universe, take my place in it, and the next day my heart beats impossibly hard when I see the photos of the comet taken by the Giotto probe, its dazzling nucleus in the shape of a peanut or a canoe, its halo of spume, its powdery trace.

Come with me, I want to show you something. I followed Ariane out back behind the house, and we started up the path on the hill – she was walking fast, her jeans floating around her bony legs, and breathing hard, as though she were hollow. At the top we were in a grassy field, and after a minute or two, she stepped away so I could see a circular mark about seven meters in diameter, stamped with six holes – the legs of the craft, is all she said. The grass was burned on top, but this wasn't from a fire, it was something else. An undefinable odor emanated from it, something like sulphur and metal powder. The circle was so perfect it could have been drawn with a compass on the ground. I had never seen this, such a clear trace. This is where they landed. Ariane raised her eyes toward me, matte, aniline, and this time I didn't look away. She went on, very distinctly: they contacted me. I thought of TFSNAP – a testimony was only kept if its consistency was judged to be superior to its strangeness, two fundamental notions, and so I took dozens of photos, kneeling in the grass, and gathered all sorts of samples. And then, putting away my equipment, I asked Ariane if she was the only one to have seen what she had seen. She was smoking again, eyes far off, and she shrugged. They're coming back tonight, do you want to wait for them with me? My eyes went back and forth between her extraordinary face and the mark on the ground. The consistency and the strangeness. I said yes.

# Translator's Note

Maylis was beginning to write these stories about voices just as the first mandates caused mouths to disappear, and I was revising the English version of *Canoes* in September 2022, when my twins saw their Kindergarten teacher's unmasked face for the first time.

This text has been held within two bodies, and taken on the inflections of two authorial voices, Maylis's in French and mine in English. In the way of literary translators, I have walked through the corridors of her text, listening intently, and have tried to match my timbre to hers as closely as two different languages and two separate worlds of reference allow.